P9-CJH-175

Stories to Tell a Five-Year-Old

Stories to Tell a Five-Year-Old

Selected by **Alice Low**

Illustrated by
Heather Harms Maione

Albany County
Public Library
Laramie, Wyoming

Little, Brown and Company

BOSTON   NEW YORK   TORONTO   LONDON

To Joanne – for Ben, Max, and Meara

A.L.

Text compilation copyright © 1996 by Alice Low
Illustrations copyright © 1996 by Heather Harms Maione

All rights reserved. No part of this book may be reproduced in any form or
by any electronic or mechanical means, including information storage
and retrieval systems, without permission in writing from the publisher,
except by a reviewer who may quote brief passages in a review.

First Edition

Copyright acknowledgments appear on page 149.

Library of Congress Cataloging-in-Publication Data
Stories to tell a five-year-old / selected by Alice Low. — 1st ed.
    p.   cm.
    Summary: A collection of more than twenty stories including folk and
fairy tale favorites, contemporary stories about everyday life, and excerpts
from childhood classics.
    ISBN 0-316-53416-1
    1. Children's stories.   [1. Short stories.]   I. Low, Alice.
PZ5.S8846 1996   95-31657
[E] — dc20

                10 9 8 7 6 5 4 3 2 1
                            MV-NY

Published simultaneously in Canada by Little, Brown & Company (Canada) Limited
Printed in the United States of America

CONTENTS

✦ Stories of Magic and Adventure ✦

✦ Stories of You and Me ✦

✦ Stories of ✦
Magic and Adventure

Molly Whuppie

Retold by Alice Low

Can plucky Molly Whuppie outwit the frightful giant? Find out in this exciting folktale from Britain.

Once upon a time, there lived a husband and wife who were so poor that they couldn't feed all of their many children. So they took their three youngest daughters and left them in the woods to fend for themselves. The three sisters walked and walked, but never a house did they see. Soon it grew dark, and oh, how hungry they were! At last they saw a light and ran toward it. To their relief, it turned out to be a house.

They knocked on the door, and a woman opened it, saying, "What do you want?"

"Please let us in and give us something to eat," said Molly Whuppie, the youngest but boldest of the three.

The woman answered, "I can't do that, as my husband is a giant, and he will kill you if he comes home and finds you here."

"Let us come in for just a little while," begged Molly, "and we will go away before he comes."

3

So the woman took them in, and set them down by the fire, and gave them milk and bread. But just as they had begun to eat, there was a great knock on the door, and a dreadful voice said,

"Fee, fie, fo, fum,
I smell the blood of some earthly one.

"Who have you got there, wife?"

"Oh," said the wife, "it's three poor lassies who are cold and hungry, but they are leaving soon. Don't touch them, my husband."

The giant said nothing but ate a big supper. Then he ordered the three children to stay all night and said that they must sleep in the same bed as his own three daughters.

Molly noticed that before she and her sisters went to bed, the giant put straw ropes around their necks, but around his own daughters' necks he put gold chains. So Molly, who was very clever, knew that the giant meant to harm her and her sisters and took care not to fall asleep. When she was sure that everyone else was sleeping soundly, she slipped out of the bed. She took the straw ropes off her own and her sisters' necks and took the gold chains off the giant's daughters. She then put the straw ropes on the giant's lassies and the gold on herself and her sisters and lay down.

And in the middle of the night, up rose the giant and felt for the necks with the straw ropes around them, for it was too dark to see. He grabbed the ropes and dragged those three, who were his own daughters, out of bed. Then he opened a trapdoor hidden in the floor and threw them in. After that, he lay down again, thinking he was well rid of his three visitors.

Molly thought it was time to be off and away, so she woke her sisters, whispered to them to be quiet, and led them out of the

4

house. They ran and ran and never stopped until morning, when they saw a grand house in front of them.

It turned out to be a palace, and Molly went in and told her story to the king. He said, "Well, Molly, you are a clever girl, and you have managed well, but if you would manage even better, and go back and steal the giant's sword that hangs on the wall behind his bed, I would give your eldest sister my eldest son to marry."

Molly said, "I'll try."

So she went back, and slipped into the giant's house, and crawled under the giant's bed. The giant came home and ate a great supper and went to sleep. Molly waited until he was snoring. Then she crept out, reached over the giant, and got down the sword.

But just as she got it out over the bed, it gave a great rattle, and up jumped the giant. Molly ran out the door, clutching the sword, and she ran, and he ran, till they came to the Bridge of One Hair. And she got over, but he couldn't, and he called out,

"Woe unto you, Molly Whuppie!
Never you come again."

And she called back,

"Twice more
I'll come to Spain."

Then Molly took the sword to the king, and her eldest sister was married to his eldest son.

"Well," the king said, "you've managed well, Molly, but if you would manage even better, and steal the purse from under the giant's pillow, I would marry your second sister to my second son."

"I'll try," said Molly.

So she set out for the giant's house, slipped in, and hid under the bed again. She waited till the giant had eaten his supper and was snoring, sound asleep. Then she crawled out, slipped her hand under the pillow, and took out the giant's purse.

But just as she was creeping away, the giant awoke and ran after her, and she ran, and he ran, till they came to the Bridge of One Hair. And she got over, but he couldn't, and he called out,

"Woe unto you, Molly Whuppie!
Never you come again."

And she called back,

"Once more
I'll come to Spain."

So Molly took the purse to the king, and her second sister was married to the king's second son.

After that, the king said to Molly, "Molly, you are a clever girl, but if you would do better yet, and steal the giant's ring that he wears on his finger, I will give you my youngest son for yourself."

Molly said she would try.

So back she went to the giant's house and hid herself under the bed. It wasn't long before the giant came home, and, after he had eaten a great big supper, he went to bed and soon was snoring loudly. Molly crept out, reached over the bed, and took hold of the giant's hand. She pulled and she pulled until she got off the ring. But just as she got it off, the giant woke up, gripped her by the hand, and said, "Now I have caught you, Molly Whuppie, and if I had treated you as you have treated me, what would you do to me?"

Molly said, "I would put you into a sack, and I'd put the cat and the dog inside with you, and a needle and thread and scissors, and I'd hang you on the wall. Then I'd go into the woods and choose the thickest stick I could get, and I'd come home, and take you down, and bang the sack till you were dead."

"Well, Molly," said the giant, "I'll do just that to you!"

So he got the sack and put Molly into it, with the cat and the dog beside her, and a needle and thread and scissors, and hung her on the wall, and went to the woods to choose a stick.

From inside the sack, Molly could hear the giant's wife working nearby. She sang out, "Oh, if only you could see what I see!"

The giant's wife begged Molly to take her up into the sack so she could see what Molly saw. So Molly took the scissors and cut a hole in the sack, and took out the needle and thread with her. Then she jumped down, helped the giant's wife up into the sack, and sewed up the hole.

The giant's wife saw nothing inside the sack and asked to be let out. But Molly didn't answer her and hid herself behind the door. Home came the giant with a great big tree in his hand, and he took down the sack and began to batter it. His wife cried out, "It's me, husband," but the dog barked and the cat mewed, and the giant could not make out his wife's voice.

Then Molly came out from behind the door, and the giant saw her and ran after her. And he ran, and she ran, till they came to the Bridge of One Hair, and she got over it, but he couldn't. And he called out,

> *"Woe unto you, Molly Whuppie!*
> *Never you come again."*

And she called back,

> *"Never more*
> *Will I come again to Spain."*

So Molly took the ring to the king, and she was married to the youngest son. And she never saw the giant again.

Puddleby and Animal Language

by Hugh Lofting

Doctor Dolittle has always loved taking care of animals. But he never knew he could learn from them. . . . Find out what Polynesia the parrot and the Doctor's other animal friends teach him in these two chapters from The Story of Doctor Dolittle.

Puddleby

Once upon a time, many years ago — when our grandfathers were little children — there was a doctor, and his name was Dolittle — John Dolittle, M.D. "M.D." means that he was a proper doctor and knew a whole lot.

He lived in a little town called Puddleby-on-the-Marsh. All the folks, young and old, knew him well by sight. And whenever he walked down the street in his high hat, everyone would say, "There goes the Doctor! He's a clever man." And the dogs and the children would all run up and follow behind him; and even the crows that lived in the church-tower would caw and nod their heads.

The house he lived in, on the edge of the town, was quite small; but his garden was very large and had a wide lawn and stone seats and weeping willows hanging over. His sister, Sarah Dolittle, was housekeeper for him; but the Doctor looked after the garden himself.

He was very fond of animals and kept many kinds of pets. Besides the goldfish in the pond at the bottom of his garden, he had rabbits in the pantry, white mice in his piano, a squirrel in the linen closet, and a hedgehog in the cellar. He had a cow with a calf, too, and an old lame horse — twenty-five years of age — and chickens and pigeons and two lambs and many other animals. But his favorite pets were Dab-Dab the duck, Jip the dog, Gub-Gub the baby pig, Polynesia the parrot, and the owl Too-Too.

His sister used to grumble about all these animals and said they made the house untidy. And one day when an old lady with rheumatism came to see the Doctor, she sat on the hedgehog, who was sleeping on the sofa, and never came to see him anymore, but drove every Saturday all the way to Oxenthorpe, another town ten miles off, to see a different doctor.

Then his sister, Sarah Dolittle, came to him and said, "John, how can you expect sick people to come and see you when you keep all these animals in the house? It's a fine doctor would have his parlor full of hedgehogs and mice! That's the fourth personage these animals have driven away. Squire Jenkins and the Parson say they wouldn't come near your house again — no matter how sick they are. We are getting poorer every day. If you go on like this, none of the best people will have you for a doctor."

"But I like the animals better than the 'best people,' " said the Doctor.

"You are ridiculous," said his sister, and walked out of the room.

So, as time went on, the Doctor got more and more animals; and the people who came to see him got less and less. Till at last he had no one left — except the Cat's-Meat-Man, who didn't mind any kind of animals. But the Cat's-Meat-Man wasn't very rich and he only got sick once a year — at Christmastime, when he used to give the Doctor sixpence for a bottle of medicine.

Sixpence a year wasn't enough to live on — even in those days, long ago; and if the Doctor hadn't had some money saved up in his money-box, no one knows what would have happened.

And he kept on getting still more pets; and of course it cost a lot to feed them. And the money he had saved up grew littler and littler.

Then he sold his piano and let the mice live in a bureau

drawer. But the money he got for that too began to go, so he sold the brown suit he wore on Sundays and went on becoming poorer and poorer.

And now, when he walked down the street in his high hat, people would say to one another, "There goes John Dolittle, M.D.! There was a time when he was the best-known doctor in the West Country. Look at him now — he hasn't any money and his stockings are full of holes!"

But the dogs and the cats and the children still ran up and followed him through the town — the same as they had done when he was rich.

Animal Language

It happened one day that the Doctor was sitting in his kitchen talking with the Cat's-Meat-Man, who had come to see him with a stomachache.

"Why don't you give up being a people's doctor and be an animal doctor?" asked the Cat's-Meat-Man.

The parrot, Polynesia, was sitting in the window looking out at the rain and singing a sailor song to herself. She stopped singing and started to listen.

"You see, Doctor," the Cat's-Meat-Man went on, "you know all about animals — much more than what these-here vets do. That book you wrote — about cats — why, it's wonderful! I can't read or write myself — or maybe *I'd* write some books. But my wife, Theodosia, she's a scholar, she is. And she read your book to me. Well, it's wonderful — that's all can be said — wonderful. You might have been a cat yourself. You know the way they think. And listen: You can make a lot of money doctoring animals. Do you know that? You see, I'd send all the old women who had sick cats or dogs to you. And if they didn't get sick fast enough, I could put something in the meat I sell 'em to make 'em sick, see?"

"Oh, no," said the Doctor quickly. "You mustn't do that. That wouldn't be right."

"Oh, I didn't mean real sick," answered the Cat's-Meat-Man. "Just a little something to make them droopy-like was what I had reference to. But as you say, maybe it ain't quite fair on the animals. But they'll get sick anyway, because the old women always give 'em too much to eat. And look, all the farmers 'round about who had lame horses and weak lambs — they'd come. Be an animal doctor."

When the Cat's-Meat-Man had gone, the parrot flew off the window onto the Doctor's table and said, "That man's got sense. That's what you ought to do. Be an animal doctor. Give the silly people up — if they haven't brains enough to see you're the best doctor in the world. Take care of animals instead — *they*'ll soon find it out. Be an animal doctor."

"Oh, there are plenty of animal doctors," said John Dolittle, putting the flowerpots outside on the windowsill to get the rain.

"Yes, there *are* plenty," said Polynesia. "But none of them are any good at all. Now listen, Doctor, and I'll tell you something. Did you know that animals can talk?"

"I knew that parrots can talk," said the Doctor.

"Oh, we parrots can talk in two languages — people's language and bird language," said Polynesia proudly. "If I say, 'Polly wants a cracker,' you understand me. But hear this: *Ka-ka oi-ee, fee-fee?*"

"Good gracious!" cried the Doctor. "What does that mean?"

"That means, 'Is the porridge hot yet?' — in bird language."

"My! You don't say so!" said the Doctor. "You never talked that way to me before."

"What would have been the good?" said Polynesia, dusting some cracker crumbs off her left wing. "You wouldn't have understood me if I had."

"Tell me some more," said the Doctor, all excited; and he rushed over to the dresser drawer and came back with the butcher's book and a pencil. "Now don't go too fast — and I'll write it down. This is interesting — very interesting — something quite new. Give me the birds' ABC first — slowly now."

15

So that was the way the Doctor came to know that animals had a language of their own and could talk to one another. And all that afternoon, while it was raining, Polynesia sat on the kitchen table giving him bird words to put down in the book.

At teatime, when the dog, Jip, came in, the parrot said to the Doctor, "See, *he's* talking to you."

"Looks to me as though he were scratching his ear," said the Doctor.

"But animals don't always speak with their mouths," said the parrot in a high voice, raising her eyebrows. "They talk with their ears, with their feet, with their tails — with everything. Sometimes they don't *want* to make a noise. Do you see now the way he's twitching up one side of his nose?"

"What's that mean?" asked the Doctor.

"That means, 'Can't you see that it has stopped raining?'" Polynesia answered. "He is asking you a question. Dogs nearly always use their noses for asking questions."

After a while, with the parrot's help, the Doctor got to learn the language of the animals so well that he could talk to them himself and understand everything they said. Then he gave up being a people's doctor altogether.

As soon as the Cat's-Meat-Man had told everyone that John Dolittle was going to become an animal doctor, old ladies began to bring him their pet pugs and poodles who had eaten too much cake, and farmers came many miles to show him sick cows and sheep.

One day a plow horse was brought to him, and the poor thing was terribly glad to find a man who could talk in horse language.

"You know, Doctor," said the horse, "that vet over the hill knows nothing at all. He has been treating me six weeks now — for spavins. What I need is *spectacles*. I am going blind in one eye. There's no reason why horses shouldn't wear glasses, the same as people.

But that stupid man over the hill never even looked at my eyes. He kept on giving me big pills. I tried to tell him, but he couldn't understand a word of horse language. What I need is spectacles."

"Of course — of course," said the Doctor. "I'll get you some at once."

"I would like a pair like yours," said the horse, "only green. They'll keep the sun out of my eyes while I'm plowing the Fifty-Acre Field."

"Certainly," said the Doctor. "Green ones you shall have."

"You know, the trouble is, sir," said the plow horse as the Doctor opened the front door to let him out — "the trouble is that *anybody* thinks he can doctor animals — just because the animals don't complain. As a matter of fact it takes a much cleverer man to be a really good animal doctor than it does to be a good people's doctor. My farmer's boy thinks he knows all about horses. He has got as much brain as a potato bug. He tried to put a mustard plaster on me last week."

"Where did he put it?" asked the Doctor.

"Oh, he didn't put it anywhere — on me," said the horse. "He only tried to. I kicked him into the duck pond."

"Well, well!" said the Doctor.

"I'm a pretty quiet creature as a rule," said the horse — "very patient with people — don't make much fuss. But it was bad enough to have that vet giving me the wrong medicine. And when that red-faced booby started to monkey with me, I just couldn't bear it anymore."

"Did you hurt the boy much?" asked the Doctor.

"Oh, no," said the horse. "I kicked him in the right place. The vet's looking after him now. When will my glasses be ready?"

"I'll have them for you next week," said the Doctor. "Come in again Tuesday — good morning!"

17

Then John Dolittle got a fine, big pair of green spectacles; and the plow horse stopped going blind in one eye and could see as well as ever.

And soon it became a common sight to see farm animals wearing glasses in the country round Puddleby; and a blind horse was a thing unknown.

And so it was with all the other animals that were brought to him. As soon as they found that he could talk their language, they told him where the pain was and how they felt, and of course it was easy for him to cure them.

Now all these animals went back and told their brothers and friends that there was a doctor in the little house with the big garden who really *was* a doctor. And whenever any creatures got sick — not only horses and cows and dogs — but all the little things of the fields, like harvest mice and water voles, badgers and bats, they came at once to his house on the edge of the town, so that his big garden was nearly always crowded with animals trying to get in to see him.

There were so many that came that he had to have special doors made for the different kinds. He wrote HORSES over the front door, COWS over the side door, and SHEEP on the kitchen door. Each kind of animal had a separate door — even the mice had a tiny tunnel made for them into the cellar, where they waited patiently in rows for the Doctor to come round to them.

And so, in a few years' time, every living thing for miles and miles got to know about John Dolittle, M.D. And the birds who flew to other countries in the winter told the animals in foreign lands of the wonderful doctor of Puddleby-on-the-Marsh, who could understand their talk and help them in their troubles. In this way he became famous among the animals — all over the world — better known even than he had been among the folks of the West Country. And he was happy and liked his life very much.

Clever Elsie

Retold by Wanda Gág

Just how clever is Elsie? Find out in this silly story from the Brothers Grimm.

There was a man, he had a daughter who always tried to use her brains as much as possible and so she was called Clever Elsie.

When she grew up, her father said, "It is time to get her married."

And his wife said, "Yes, if only someone would come along who might want her."

At last from far away came one by name of Hans, who said, "Yes, I'll marry the girl, but only if she's really as clever as you say."

"Oh," said the father, "our Elsie is no fool."

And the mother said, "Ei, that's true. She is so clever, she can see the wind coming up the street. Yes, and she can hear the flies cough, too."

"Well, we'll see," said Hans, "but if she's not bright I don't want her."

After they had all sat down at the table and had eaten something, the mother said, "Elsie, go down into the cellar and get us some cider."

At this the clever girl took the jug from the wall and trotted down the cellar stairs, clattering the lid smartly on the way, so as to be doing something with her time. Down in the cellar she brought out a little stool, put it in front of the cask, and sat on it, so she wouldn't have to bend over and perhaps unexpectedly hurt her back. Then she set the jug in front of the cask and turned on the tap. But while she was waiting for the jug to be filled, she did not want her eyes to remain idle, so she began busily looking around at the walls and ceiling. After much gazing hither and thither, what should she see right above her but a pickax which had been forgotten and left there by the masons! At this, Clever Elsie burst into tears, thinking: "If I should marry Hans and we should get a little baby, and he grows up and we send him down here to draw some cider, that pickax might suddenly fall down on his head and kill him."

So there she sat and cried with all her might over this possible accident.

Those up in the kitchen waited and waited for her, but she did not, did not come. At last the mother said to the hired girl, "Do go down into the cellar and see what's keeping our Clever Elsie."

When the girl went down and found Elsie sitting there, weeping so bitterly, she said, "Why are you crying like that?"

"Ach!" said Elsie. "Why shouldn't I cry? If I marry Hans and we get a baby and he's grown up and comes down here to draw some cider, maybe that pickax will fall on his head and kill him."

At this the hired girl said, "How can you think of all those

21

things? Oh, what a clever Elsie you are, to be sure." So she sat down beside Elsie and began to cry, too, over the great misfortune.

After a time, as the hired girl did not return and those up in the kitchen were becoming restless and thirsty, the father said to the hired man, "You! Do you go down into the cellar and see what is keeping Elsie and the hired girl."

The hired man went down. There sat the two girls, both crying as though their hearts would break.

"What are you crying about, then?" asked the hired man.

"Ach!" said Elsie. "Why shouldn't we cry? When I marry Hans and we get a child and he's grown up and has to come down here and draw cider, this pickax might easily fall down on his head and kill him."

"Oh, what a calamity!" cried the hired man. "And what a clever Elsie you are, to be sure." So he sat down too, and kept them company with loud and anguished howls.

Above in the kitchen, the others were waiting for the hired man. As he didn't come and didn't come, the father said to the mother, "Wife, do you go down into the cellar and see where our Clever Elsie is staying."

The mother went down and found all three in the midst of loud lamentations. When she asked them the reason for such grief, Elsie explained that her future child would surely be killed, in case he should come down to draw cider just as the pickax might fall down on his head.

"Oh!" said the mother. "Who but our Clever Elsie could think so far ahead?" And she sat down and joined the rest in their sobs and howls.

The father up in the kitchen waited a while for his wife, but as she did not return either, he said, "Well, I guess I'll have to go down there myself and see what is keeping our Clever Elsie so long."

As he went down the cellar stairs and saw all four sitting there and crying, he asked them what was the matter. And when he heard that the reason for their grief was a child which Elsie might have someday, and which might be killed in case the pickax should fall down just at the time the child might be sitting there drawing cider, he cried, "Ah! That is foresight indeed! What a clever Elsie we have, to be sure." And he sat down and cried, too.

Hans, in the meantime, stayed up in the kitchen for a long time, but as no one returned, he said to himself, "They'll be waiting for you down there, no doubt. You'd better go down and see what they're about."

As he went down into the cellar there sat the five, moaning and howling pitifully, one always louder than the next.

"What terrible misfortune has happened down here?" cried Hans.

"Ach, dear Hans!" wept Elsie. "If you and I get married and have a baby and he grows up and we might perhaps send him down here to draw some cider, that pickax might fall on his head and kill him. Isn't that something to cry about?"

"Well!" cried Hans. "That shows deep thought. More wisdom than this is not needful for my household, and, since you are really such a clever Elsie, I will marry you!"

He grabbed her by the hand, took her upstairs, and soon they were celebrating their wedding.

After Hans and Elsie were married and had a house and farm of their own, Hans said, "Wife, I must go out and earn some money. Do you go off into the field and reap the rye so that we may have bread."

"Yes, yes, dear Hans, that I will do," said Clever Elsie.

After he had gone, she cooked up a good big broth and took it with her to the field. Once there, she sat down and began to use her brain as usual, for she wanted to be sure not to do the wrong thing. So she asked herself, "What shall I do? Shall I eat before I reap? Or shall I sleep before I reap? Hei! I'll eat first."

She sat down and ate up all the broth, and this made her almost too drowsy to move.

"I must put my clever brain to work," she thought to herself. "Now then, shall I sleep first or shall I reap first? Shall I reap or shall I sleep?" And so as not to waste any time while she was thinking, she began to cut down the grain.

She was now so sleepy she hardly knew what she was doing. While she was still saying, "Shall I reap? Shall I sleep? Reap or sleep? Sleep? Reap?" she began to cut off her clothes, thinking it was the rye. Apron, shirt, skirt, and kirtle: all were slashed in half.

But Elsie did not know it — she was still asking herself the big question, "Shall I reap first or sleep first?"

At last she found the answer. "Hei, I'll sleep first!" she said, tumbled down among the rye stalks, and was soon sleeping soundly.

When she awoke it was almost dark. She got up, and seeing herself all tattered and torn, and half naked besides, she did not know herself.

"I wonder," she said, "am I, I? Or am I not I?"

Try as she would, she couldn't find the answer, so she went on, "Now you! You're very clever and you ought to know. Think hard! Are you Elsie or somebody else?"

Still she didn't know.

At last the clever girl had an idea. "I know!" she said. "I'll go home and see if I'm there or not."

So she ran home and knocked at the window and said, "Is Clever Elsie there?"

"Yes, yes," said Hans, who thought she had come home long ago, "no doubt she's in her bed fast asleep."

"Ach!" cried Clever Elsie. "Then I'm already at home, and this is not I and I'm not Elsie but somebody else, and I don't live here."

So she ran away, and no one ever saw her after that. But as she was such a clever girl and always knew what to do, I'm sure she got along very well wherever she went.

The Miller, His Son, and Their Donkey

Adapted from the fables of Aesop
by Joseph Jacobs

Aesop's fables are among the oldest and best-loved stories in the world. This famous tale tells what happens when a man and his son try too hard to please everyone they meet. . . .

A miller, accompanied by his young son, was taking his donkey to market in hopes of finding a purchaser for him. On the road they met a troop of girls, laughing and talking, who exclaimed, "Did you ever see such a pair of fools? To be trudging along the dusty road when they might be riding!"

The miller thought there was sense in what they said; so he made his son mount the donkey, and himself walked at the side.

Presently they met some of his old cronies, who greeted them and said, "You'll spoil that son of yours, letting him ride while you toil along on foot! Make him walk, young lazybones! It'll do him all the good in the world."

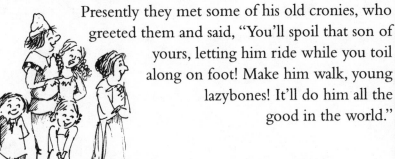

The miller followed their advice, and took his son's place on the back of the donkey while the boy trudged along behind. They had not gone far when they overtook a party of women and children, and the miller heard them say, "What a selfish old man! He himself rides in comfort, but lets his poor little boy follow as best he can on his own legs!" So he made his son get up behind him. Farther along the road they met some travelers, who asked the miller whether the donkey he was riding was his own property or a beast hired for the occasion. He replied that it was his own and that he was taking it to market to sell.

"Good heavens!" said they. "With a load like that the poor beast will be so exhausted by the time he gets there that no one will look at him. Why, you'd do better to carry him!" "Anything to please you," said the old man. "We can but try." So they got off, tied the donkey's legs together with a rope, and slung him on a pole, and at last reached the town, carrying him between them. This was so absurd a sight that the people ran out in crowds to laugh at it, and mocked the father and son unmercifully. They had then got to a bridge over the river where the donkey, frightened by the noise and his unusual situation, kicked and struggled till he broke the ropes that bound him, fell into the water, and floated far, far away. Whereupon the unfortunate miller, vexed and ashamed, made his way home again, convinced that in trying to please all he had pleased none, and had lost his donkey in the bargain.

Rumpelstiltskin

Retold by Virginia Haviland

A funny little man offers to help a girl spin straw into gold — but what will he want in return? A fairy tale favorite from the Brothers Grimm.

There was once a miller who was very poor, but he had a very beautiful daughter.

It happened, one day, that this miller was talking with the king. To make himself seem important, he told the king that he had a daughter who could spin gold out of straw.

The king answered, "That would suit me well. If your daughter is as clever as you say, bring her to my castle tomorrow, so that I may see for myself what she can do."

When the girl was brought to him, he led her into a room that was full of straw. He gave her a wheel and spindle, and said, "Now set to work. If by early morning you have not spun this straw to gold, you shall die."

He locked the door and left her alone.

And so the poor miller's daughter sat. For the life of her, she could not think what to do. She had no idea how to spin gold from straw. Her plight was so hopeless that she began to weep.

Then all at once the door opened. In came a little man, who said, "Good evening, miller's daughter; why are you crying?"

"Oh," answered the girl, "I have to spin gold out of straw — and I don't know how to do it."

The little man asked, "What will you give me if I spin it for you?"

"My necklace," answered the girl.

The little man took the necklace. He sat down before the wheel, and — *whirr, whirr, whirr!* — three times around, and the bobbin was full of gold. Then he took up another, and — *whirr,*

whirr, whirr! — three times around, and that one was full. So he went on till the morning, when all the straw was spun and all the bobbins were full of gold.

At sunrise, in came the king. When he saw the gold, he was astonished — and very pleased, for he was greedy. He had the miller's daughter taken into another room filled with straw, much bigger than the last. He told her that if she wanted to live she must spin all this in one night.

Again the girl did not know what to do, so she began to cry. The door opened, and the same little man appeared as before. He asked, "What will you give me if I spin all this straw into gold?"

"The ring from my finger," answered the girl.

So the little man took the ring, and began again to send the wheel whirring around.

By the next morning all the straw was spun into glittering gold. The king was happy beyond words. But, as he could never have enough gold, he had the miller's daughter taken into a still larger room full of straw, and said, "This straw, too, you must spin in one night. If you do, you shall be my wife." He thought to himself, "Although she is but a miller's daughter, I am not likely to find anyone richer in the whole world."

As soon as the girl was alone, the little man came for the third time and asked, "What will you give me if I spin this straw for you?"

"I have nothing left to give," answered the girl.

"Then you must promise me the first child you have after you are queen," said the little man.

"Well, who knows what may happen?" thought the girl. As she could think of nothing else to do, she promised the little man what he demanded. In return, he began to spin, and spun until all the straw was gold.

31

In the morning when the king came and found everything done as he wished, he had the wedding held at once, and the miller's pretty daughter became queen.

In a year's time, a beautiful child was born. The queen had forgotten all about the little man — until one day he came into her room suddenly and said, "Now give me what you promised me."

The queen was terrified. She offered the little man all the riches of the kingdom — if only he would leave the child.

But the little man said, "No, I would rather have a baby than all the treasures of the world."

The queen began to weep, so that the little man felt sorry for her.

"I will give you three days," he said, "and if in that time you cannot tell my name, you must give me the child."

The queen spent the whole night thinking over all the names she had ever heard. She sent a messenger through the land to ask far and wide for all the names that could be found.

When the little man came next day, she began with Caspar, Melchior, and Balthazar, and she repeated all she knew.

But after each the little man said, "No, that is not my name."

The second day the queen sent to ask all the neighbors what their servants were called. She told the little man all the most unusual names, saying, "Perhaps you are called Cow-ribs, or Sheep-shanks, or Spider-legs?"

But he answered only, "No, that is not my name."

On the third day, the messenger came back and said, "I have not been able to find one single new name. But as I passed through the woods, I came to a high hill. Near it was a little house, and before the house burned a fire. Around the fire danced a funny little man, who hopped on one leg and sang:

Tomorrow at last the child comes in,
For nobody knows I'm Rumpelstiltskin.' "

You cannot think how pleased the queen was to hear that name!

Soon the little man himself walked in and asked, "Now, Your Majesty, what is my name?"

At first she asked, "Are you called Jack?"

"No, that is not my name."

"Are you called Harry?"

"No," answered he.

And then she asked, "Perhaps your name is Rumpelstiltskin?"

"The devil told you that! The devil told you that!" shrieked the little man. In his anger he stamped with his right foot so hard that it went into the ground above his knee. Then he seized his left foot with both hands in such a fury that he split in two. And that was the end of him!

Lazy Jack

Adapted from Joseph Jacobs

Jack tries to do just exactly what his mother asks him to. So why does everything seem to turn out wrong? Find out in this old tale from England.

Once upon a time, a boy named Jack lived with his mother in a small house at the edge of town. Jack's mother earned a few coins by spinning, but she and her son were still very poor, for Jack's mother could not get him to do any work at all, even though he knew that she was growing old and could not spin as well as she once had. Jack was so lazy that he would do nothing but lie in the hot sun in the summer, and sit in the corner by the fire during wintertime. So all of the townspeople came to call him Lazy Jack.

Finally, one Monday, his mother grew so tired of his laziness that she told him that if he did not begin to work for his supper, she would turn him out of the house, and he would have to earn a living as he could.

Now, Jack's mother kept a comfortable house, and Jack did

not want to leave it. So the very next day, he went out and asked a neighboring farmer for work. As Jack walked home that evening, he tossed the single penny he had earned up in the air and caught it, over and over. But when he came to the bridge that crossed over a brook, he tossed the coin a little too high, and it flew over his shoulder and into the water.

"Dear me," cried his mother when Jack told her what had happened. "You should have put it in your pocket!"

"I promise I will next time, Mother," Jack replied.

On Wednesday, Jack went out again. This time, he found a job working for the dairyman, who gave him a jar of milk for his day's wages. Following his mother's advice, Jack took the jar and put it into the large pocket of his jacket. Daydreaming as he walked, Jack didn't notice that all the milk had spilled out of the jar long before he reached home.

"You silly fellow," said his mother when she saw what had happened. "You should have carried it on your head!"

"I promise I will next time, Mother," Jack said.

So on Thursday, Jack went to work for a farmer who lived on the opposite side of the county, who gave him a creamy cheese for his services. In the evening, Jack took the cheese, balanced it on his head, and walked slowly home. By the time he reached the cottage, the cheese was spoiled, for part of it had fallen off as he walked, and the rest was all stuck in his hair.

"You foolish boy," said his mother. "You should have carried it carefully in your hands."

"I promise I will next time, Mother," Jack said.

On Friday, Jack went out again and took a job with the baker, who would give him nothing for his work but an old tomcat.

Jack liked cats, and, following his mother's advice, he carried the old tom carefully in his hands. But the cat didn't want to leave his home, and he scratched Jack until the boy was forced to let him go.

When he got home and told his mother what had happened, she said to him, "You ninny, you should have tied it with a string and led it home behind you."

"I promise I will next time, Mother," Jack said.

So on Saturday, Jack hired himself out to the butcher. The butcher rewarded Jack with a handsome roast. Jack, mindful of his mother's words, took a string and tied it to the roast, and dragged it all the way home. When his mother came out and saw what would have been her Sunday dinner all covered in dirt, she grew quite out of patience with her foolish son. "You stupid boy, you should have carried it on your shoulders!"

"I promise I will next time, Mother," Jack told her.

And so after a Sunday dinner of only cabbage, Jack went out on the next Monday and found a job working for a cattleman. In return, the cattleman gave Jack a donkey. Jack, remembering his promise to his mother, didn't ride the donkey; he hoisted it over his shoulders instead!

It took Jack a long while to get home this way, for the donkey was very heavy and kept falling off his back. It was just starting to get dark when he walked by the home of the wealthiest family in the town. The daughter of this family was very beautiful, but she had not been able to speak since she was a little girl. She had never laughed in all her life, either, and the doctors all said that she would never speak until someone had first made her laugh.

Now, when Jack saw the pretty girl sitting in the window, he smiled, and bowed to her, and tried to take off his cap. But his hands were busy holding up the donkey, and whenever he tried to free one to reach for his hat, one of the donkey's legs would start to slide down his back, and he'd have to hurry to grab it before the whole animal fell to the ground.

Well, the sight of Jack with the donkey on his back, its legs sticking up every which way, was so strange and funny that the beautiful girl in the window burst out in a great fit of laughter. She laughed and laughed, until her sides ached from it. Finally, when she could laugh no longer, she came down and began to talk to Jack, for the laughter had loosened her tongue, and she could now speak freely.

The girl's wealthy parents were overjoyed to see their daughter laughing and talking again. They granted her wish that she be married to the man who had made her laugh, and Lazy Jack was made a rich gentleman. Jack and his wife lived in a grand new house. Jack's mother lived with them there, and never had to worry about her silly, lazy son again.

The Sorcerer's Apprentice

Retold by Barbara Shook Hazen

Humboldt is certain that casting a spell to clean the sorcerer's house will be much easier than doing the work himself. But if you're going to use magic, you'd better know what you're doing. . . . Based on an old German poem.

Long, long ago there lived a sorcerer — a wise old wizard — who could weave the most marvelous magic spells. He could turn princes into field mice, pebbles into pure gold, and he could make himself disappear — *Presto!* — in a puff of pale blue powder.

The sorcerer lived in a castle high above the River Rhine. The castle had tall towers, twisted turrets, and a maze of vaulted passageways which led to a deep, dank cellar.

The cellar was the sorcerer's workshop. One side of the cellar was lined with shelves of musty, dusty, leather-bound books. By far the most important book of all was an enormous volume called *Complete Magic Spells and Incantations*. It contained the sorcerer's secrets: all his charms and conjurations, all his rites and rituals, and all his symbols and secret words.

This book stood alone on the top shelf, where it was guarded day and night by an old green-eyed owl. The book was always locked, and the sorcerer always wore the key around his neck.

On the other side of the cellar was the sorcerer's laboratory. There stood the sorcerer's kiln, his cosmic oven, and the distillery where he made secret chemical concoctions. And there, too, were all the other tools of the sorcerer's trade: cauldrons and kettles, flagons and flasks, alantirs and ampulars, bubbling beakers and vapor-filled vessels — and piles of phosphorescent stones ready to be pulverized into magic powders and potions.

In the middle of the workshop was a water tub. Every day the tub had to be filled. Heavy buckets of water had to be brought all the way up the steep stone steps which led from the River Rhine.

Carrying all those heavy buckets was the job of the sorcerer's apprentice — a frisky, likeable, but sometimes lazy lad named Humboldt.

Humboldt wanted to be a sorcerer, too, someday, and so he worked at the castle in return for lessons in magic. Humboldt loved the lessons, but he hated the chores. He hated the sweeping and cleaning and rubbing and scrubbing. Most of all, he hated having to carry bucket after bucket of water up the steep stone steps.

Humboldt preferred to skip and sing, to chase squirrels or play with the sorcerer's cat — or just to sit by the riverbank, daydreaming and watching the beautiful Rhine flow through the countryside.

The sorcerer knew this, for he was wise in the ways of lazy boys. And whenever he caught Humboldt loafing or napping or making up excuses, the sorcerer made him work twice as hard.

None of Humboldt's mumbling or grumbling could change the sorcerer's mind. "An apprentice must work. An apprentice must learn. An apprentice must *earn* his magic powers," said the sorcerer. "Magic is a powerful tool, my boy — far too powerful to use unless you know how to use it wisely. Sorcery is far more than casting a spell. You will see — someday."

One day the sorcerer was called to a meeting in the Black Forest. Before going, he climbed the library ladder and copied some words out of the big book of magic.

Then he said to Humboldt, "All the wizards and wise men from far and near have called a conclave. I must join them. While I am gone, guard the castle and do your tasks. When I return, I expect to see all the cauldrons scrubbed, all the brass beakers rubbed, and not one speck of dirt upon the floor. Most important, I expect to find the water tub filled all the way up — to the *brim,* Humboldt! And I don't expect you to stop working till you've finished *all* your chores!"

Then the sorcerer covered himself with his cloak and mumbled a few magic words, and disappeared — *Pfffffft!* — in a puff of pale blue powder — which promptly settled all over the furniture and the floor.

"As if things aren't bad enough," grumbled Humboldt, "he makes more work for me. It isn't fair. He has all the fun and I do all the dirty work. Why should I slave all day when the master could cast one magic spell and have all the chores done in an instant? Magic's a much easier way, and much more fun, too!"

Hopelessly, Humboldt looked around at the dirt and dust, and as he looked, a shiny object caught his eye.

There on the sorcerer's worktable was the gold key to the big book of magic. The sorcerer had been in such a hurry, he had forgotten it. What luck!

Humboldt grabbed the key. Then he looked at the top library shelf to make sure the old owl was asleep. It was.

Quickly, Humboldt steadied the library ladder and climbed to the top. His hands shook with excitement as he unlocked the big red-and-gold book. Making as little noise as possible, Humboldt flipped through the parchment pages. There were circles and

stars and mysterious symbols. Most of the words were in a language Humboldt couldn't understand.

Then he saw, under the heading PRACTICAL MAGIC, *Broom, magic: How to make a stick fulfill all the wishes of your will.*

"That means the broom will do anything I ask," thought Humboldt happily. So he said the words over and over till he knew them by heart.

Then he closed the book, fastened his eyes on the old straw broom in the corner of the cellar, and called out:

> *"SHARRRROOM TA!*
> *VARRRROOM BA!*
> *Old broom perk,*
> *Bring water*
> *And do all my work."*

Hearing the noise, the old owl awakened with a flurry and a flapping of wings, and batted the boy off the ladder.

The ladder crashed and broke in two. But luckily Humboldt landed unhurt, cushioned by the sorcerer's stuffed crocodile.

Humboldt lay there stunned. At first nothing happened. Had he said the wrong magic words?

No! Look! The broom moved.

Then it flipped on its end. Hop. Hop.

Hooray! The magic words were right. The broom was beginning to work.

Humboldt pointed to a water bucket.

Hop. Hop. The broom hopped over, bent, and picked up the bucket. Then it hopped across the cellar floor, out the castle door, and down the steep stone steps to the River Rhine.

At the water's edge, the broom tipped, dipped the bucket into the water, and filled it. Then it turned and hopped all the way back up the steep stone steps.

Without stopping, the broom carried the bucket into the castle and poured the water into the tub.

Then it started all over again. It hopped to the door and began hobbling and bobbling and thumping and bumping down to the riverbank.

"Hooray!" Humboldt shouted with delight. "I did it! I did it! I made the magic work for me!"

Humboldt hugged the sorcerer's cat and started dancing and singing around the room.

Humboldt kept on singing and dancing, and the broom kept on hobbling and bobbling, and the water kept on rising in the tub.

Then Humboldt forgot all about the water tub for a while. He patted the sorcerer's pet snakes and salamanders. He played marbles with the sorcerer's magic stones. He even made hot tea on the sorcerer's cosmic oven. And why not! His master was away and the work was being done. No one would even know.

All at once, Humboldt noticed that the water was up to the brim of the tub.

"Stop, broom! That's enough. Go back to your corner," he called.

But the broom didn't stop. It kept right on hopping. It kept right on thumping and bumping down the steep stone steps and back again with buckets of water. And it kept right on emptying the buckets into the tub, which by now was overflowing.

Water trickled over the rim and ran down the sides. Water drenched the rug and sloshed the floor and made a big, sloppy puddle by the cellar door. The sorcerer's cat, who hated to get her paws wet, yowled in rage.

Humboldt was frightened. "*Stop, broom!*" he cried out again. "Broom, you've *got* to stop. Do as I say, *broom. Obey!*"

But the broom *didn't* stop. It kept right on hobbling and bobbling and bringing more water.

The water rose higher and higher. The puddle by the door became a pond. The fire in the oven went out with a hiss. Only the salamanders, swimming and swishing their tails in the floodwaters, were happy.

Humboldt couldn't stop what he had started. And he couldn't look in the magic book again because the ladder was broken. He was frantic.

"Woe! Oh, misery!" he whined. "What will my master say? What will he do when he sees what I've done? Maybe he'll turn me into a toad — or throw me out — or do something terrible. Oh, why did I look in the magic book! If only I can remember some of the magic words, maybe the broom will stop."

Hoping they were like the words that had *started* the broom working, Humboldt called out:

"*SHARRRROOM TA!*
VARRRROOM BA!
Old broom stop
your hopping.
Do as I say."

Nothing happened. So he tried again:

"*SHARRRROOM TA!*
VARRRROOM BA!
Go back broom.
Stop hopping.
You must obey."

But the broom didn't stop. It kept right on hobbling and bobbling and bringing buckets of water. No *other* combination of words worked, either. Not even saying the *Varrrroom ba!* before the *Sharrrroom ta!* Not anything.

The water was now waist high. The cat was climbing the furniture, and the snakes were slithering up the draperies. Scared and soaked to the skin, Humboldt knew he had to do *some*thing to stop the broom. He grabbed the sorcerer's axe.

And when the broom came back with still another bucket of water, Humboldt lifted the axe high. *Crack! Whack!* He cut the broom in two.

The room was silent.

"Aha, broom! I've got you at last," Humboldt cried out. "Got you for good. Your magic won't get me into any more trouble."

But even as he said it, something amazing and unbelievable and horrible happened.

The two pieces of the broom quivered. Then they both tipped, flipped over, and started hopping. Then each of them picked up a bucket and went bumping and thumping down the steep stone steps to the River Rhine.

Even more awful, all the broom *splinters* did the same thing. Soon there was a procession of hundreds of brooms, big and little and in-between, all hobbling and bobbling, all thumping and bumping, all bringing buckets of water from the river.

By now the flood had reached the top shelf of the bookcase. Humboldt was swimming for his life and trying to catch the magic book, bobbing always just out of reach.

The cat and the owl were clinging to the chandelier and screeching in fury. Cauldrons were slamming, and kettles were banging. All the magic powders and potions were washed into the floodwaters, turning them pink and purple and gentian violet.

And still all the brooms kept hobbling and bobbling and bringing water.

Soon water was everywhere: whirling, swirling; curling into whirlpools; rushing, gushing, pushing the animals; drowning, surrounding, pounding the furniture.

Humboldt's fingers on the mantelpiece were slowly, steadily, slipping, slipping.

"Help!" Humboldt cried. "Help, master, I am going down. Help, master, I am going to drown!"

Suddenly there was a blinding flash of light. *Presto!* In a puff of pale blue powder, the sorcerer appeared at the top of the steps. He bellowed angrily,

> *"HALT TA!*
> *SCHTALT BA!*
> *Old broom to the corner.*
> *Cessare!"*

Slowly, the water subsided.

Slowly, Humboldt floated to the floor.

Slowly, everything became as it had been.

"Mm-mm-mm-master, it was only a joke," Humboldt muttered feebly. "Pl-pl-please don't punish me."

"Ha!" said the sorcerer, his eyes flashing fire. Then he pointed to the water bucket.

Waterlogged and bone weary, the sorcerer's apprentice walked to the corner. He bent to pick up the empty bucket.

And as Humboldt bent, the broom in the corner tipped and flipped over. *Slap! Whack! Bang! Crack!* It gave Humboldt four sharp whacks on the backside — which sent the sorcerer's apprentice flying all the way down the steep stone steps to the River Rhine.

AND THAT WAS THAT!

The Squire's Bride

Retold by James Riordan

A clever young woman plays a hilarious trick on a greedy old man in this story based on a folktale from Norway.

There was once a rich squire with a mint of silver in the barn and gold aplenty in the bank. He farmed over hill and dale, was ruddy and stout, yet he lacked a wife. So he had a mind to wed.

After all, since I am rich, he thought, I can pick and choose whatever maid I wish.

One afternoon the squire was wandering down the lane when he spotted a sturdy lass toiling in the hay field. And he rubbed his grizzled chins, muttering to himself, "Oh, aye, I fancy she'd do all right, and save me a packet on wages, too. Since she's poor and humble, she'll take my offer, right enough."

So he had her brought to the manor house, where he sat her down, all hot and flustered.

"Now then, gal," he began, "I've a mind to take a wife."

49

"Mind on, then," she said. "One may mind of much and more."

She wondered whether the old buffer had his sights set on her; why else should she be summoned?

"Aye, lass, I've picked thee out. Tha'll make a decent wife, sure enough."

"No thank you," said she, "though much obliged, I'm sure."

The squire's ruddy face turned ruby red — he was not used to people talking back. The more he blathered, the more she turned him down, and none too politely either. Yet the more she refused, the more he wanted what he could not have. With a final sigh, he dismissed the lass and sent for her father. Perhaps the man would talk some sense into his daughter's head.

"Go to it, man," the squire roared. "I'll overlook the money you owe me and give you a meadow into the bargain. What d'ye say to that?"

"Oh, aye, Squire. Be sure I'll bring her round," the father said. "Pardon her plain speaking; she's young yet and don't know what's best."

All the same, in spite of all his coaxing and bawling, the girl was adamant — she would not have the old miser even if he were made of gold! And that was that.

When the poor farmer did not return to the manor house with the girl's consent, the squire stormed and stamped impatiently. And next day he went to call on the man.

"Settle this matter right away," he ranted on, "or it'll be the worse for you. I won't bide a day longer for my bride."

There was nothing for it. Together the master and the farmer hatched a plan: the squire was to see to all the wedding chores — parson, guests, wedding feast — and the farmer would send his daughter at the appointed hour. He would say nothing of the wedding to her, but just let her think that work awaited her up at the big house.

Of course, when she arrived she would be so dazzled by the wedding dress, afeared of the parson, and awed by the guests that she would readily give her consent. How could a farm girl refuse the squire? And so it was arranged.

When all the guests had assembled at the manor and the white wedding gown laid out and the parson, in black hat and cloak, settled down, the master sent for a stable lad. "Go to the farmer," he ordered, "and bring back what I'm promised. And be back here in two ticks or I'll tan your hide!"

The lad rushed off, wondering what the promise was. In no time at all he was knocking on the farmer's door.

"My master's sent me to fetch what you promised him," panted the lad.

"Oh, aye, dare say he has," the farmer said. "She's down in the meadow. You'd better take her, then."

Off ran the lad to the meadow and found the daughter raking hay.

"I've come to fetch what your father promised the squire," he said, all out of breath.

It did not take the girl long to figure out the plot.

So that's their game, she thought, a twinkle in her eye. "All right, then, lad, you'd better take her, then. It's the old gray mare grazing over there."

With a leap and a bound the lad was on the gray mare's back and riding home at full gallop. Once there he leapt down at the door, dashed inside, and called up to the squire.

"She's at the door now, Squire."

"Well done," called down the master. "Take her up to my old mother's room."

"But master —"

"Don't but me, you scoundrel," the old codger roared. "If you can't manage her on your own, get someone else to help."

On glimpsing the squire's angry face, the lad knew it was no use arguing. So he called some farmhands and they set to work.

Some pulled the old mare's ears; others pushed her rump. They heaved and shoved until finally they got her up the stairs and into the empty room. There they tied the reins to a bedpost and let her be.

Wiping the sweat from his brow, the lad now reported to the squire.

"That's the darnedest job I've ever done," he complained.

"Now send the wenches up to dress her in the wedding gown," said the squire.

The stable lad stared.

"Get on with it, dung-head. And tell them not to forget the veil and crown. Jump to it!"

Forthwith the lad burst into the pantry to tell the news.

"Hey, listen here, go upstairs and dress the old mare in wedding clothes. That's what the master says. He must be playing a joke on his guests."

The cooks and chambermaids all but split their sides with laughter. But in the end they scrambled up the stairs and dressed the poor gray mare as if she were a bride. That done, the lad went off once more to the squire.

"Right, lad, now bring her downstairs. I'll be in the drawing room with my guests. Just throw open the door and announce the bride."

There came a noisy clatter and thumping on the stairs as the old gray mare was prodded down. At last she stood impatiently in the hallway before the door. Then, all at once, the door burst open and all the guests looked around in expectation.

What a shock they got!

In trotted the old gray mare dressed up as a bride, with a crown sprawling on one ear, veil draped over her eyes, and gown covering her rump. Seeing the crowd, she let out a fierce neigh, turned tail, and fled out of the house.

The parson spilled his glass of port all down his purple front;

the squire gaped in amazement; the guests let out a roar of laughter that could be heard for miles around.

And the squire, they say, never went courting again.

As for the girl, some say she married; some say not. It matters little. What is certain is that she lived happily ever after.

The Prince Who Thought He Was a Rooster

Retold by Howard Schwartz and Barbara Rush

*The prince thinks he is a rooster —
and acts like one, too! What a problem
for his father, the king! A humorous
Jewish folktale from Eastern Europe.*

There once was a prince who thought he was a rooster. While other princes spent their days slaying dragons, courting princesses, or learning how to rule a kingdom, this prince cast off his royal robes and spent his days crouching beneath a table, refusing to eat any food except kernels of corn.

His father, the king, was very upset at this behavior. "Send for the best doctors in all the land," he proclaimed. "A great reward will be given to anyone who can cure my son."

Doctors came from all corners of the kingdom. Each tried to cure the prince, but not one of them succeeded. The prince still thought he was a rooster. He ate corn, preened his feathers, and strutted about, crying, "Cock-a-doodle-doo! Cock-a-doodle-doo!"

When the king had almost given up hope, a wise man, passing

through the kingdom, appeared before him. "Let me stay alone with the prince for one week, and I will cure him," he said to the king.

"Everyone else has failed," the king moaned, "but you are welcome to try."

Thus the wise man entered the prince's chamber. There he took off his clothes, crawled under the table, and began to eat kernels of corn, just like the prince.

The prince looked at the man with suspicion. "Who are you?" he asked.

"I am a rooster," said the wise man, and he continued to munch the corn. After a short while he asked, "Who are you?"

"I, too, am a rooster," said the prince.

And after that the prince treated the wise man as an equal. The

two strutted about, preening their feathers and crying, "Cock-a-doodle-doo! Cock-a-doodle-doo!"

When they had made their home under the table for a while and had become good friends, the wise man suddenly crawled out into the prince's chamber and dressed himself.

The prince was shocked.

"A rooster doesn't wear clothes!" he said.

The wise man remained calm. "I am a rooster, and I am wearing clothes!"

The prince considered this for a day or two. Then he decided to imitate his friend, and he, too, put on clothes.

A few days later, the wise man took some of the food that was being delivered to them every day, food that they had refused to eat. He carried it beneath the table and ate it.

The prince was astonished. "Roosters don't eat that kind of food!"

But the wise man calmly said, "A rooster can eat any food he wants and still be a good rooster." And he continued to eat the tasty food.

The prince watched this for a while. Then he decided to imitate his friend, and he, too, ate the food.

The next day the wise man stopped crouching beneath the table. He stood up proudly on his two feet and started to walk like a man.

"What are you doing?" asked the prince. "A rooster can't get up and walk around like that!"

But the wise man said firmly, "I am a rooster, and if I want to walk like this, I will!" And he continued to walk upright.

The prince peered at him from beneath the table. Then he decided to imitate his friend, and he, too, stood up and walked on his two feet.

So, in this way, the prince began to eat, dress, and walk like a man. The week's time was up, and no longer did he act like a rooster. The king was overjoyed, of course, and welcomed his son back with open arms.

As for the wise man, why, he collected his reward and went happily on his way.

The Day Out

by P. L. Travers

*Mary Poppins can make an ordinary
day turn into a fantastic holiday. Read
all about it in this story from* Mary
Poppins, *the first book in the classic
series about a stern but magical
English nanny.*

"Every third Thursday," said Mrs. Banks. "Two till five."

Mary Poppins eyed her sternly. "The best people, ma'am," she said, "give every *second* Thursday, and one till six. And those I shall take or —" Mary Poppins paused, and Mrs. Banks knew what the pause meant. It meant that if she didn't get what she wanted Mary Poppins would not stay.

"Very well, very well," said Mrs. Banks hurriedly, though she wished Mary Poppins did not know so very much more about the best people than she did herself.

So Mary Poppins put on her white gloves and tucked her umbrella under her arm — not because it was raining but because it had such a beautiful handle that she couldn't possibly leave it at home. How could you leave your umbrella behind if it had a parrot's head for a handle? Besides, Mary Poppins was very vain and liked to look her best. Indeed, she was quite sure that she never looked anything else.

Jane waved to her from the Nursery window.

"Where are you going?" she called.

"Kindly close that window," replied Mary Poppins, and Jane's head hurriedly disappeared inside the Nursery.

Mary Poppins walked down the garden path and opened the gate. Once outside in the Lane, she set off walking very quickly as if she were afraid the afternoon would run away from her if she didn't keep up with it. At the corner she turned to the right and then to the left, nodded haughtily to the Policeman, who said it was a nice day, and by that time she felt that her Day Out had begun.

She stopped beside an empty motorcar in order to put her hat straight with the help of the windscreen, in which it was reflected, then she smoothed down her frock and tucked her umbrella more securely under her arm so that the handle, or rather the parrot, could be seen by everybody. After these preparations she went forward to meet the Match-Man.

Now, the Match-Man had two professions. He not only sold matches like any ordinary match-man, but he drew pavement pictures as well. He did these things turn-about according to the weather. If it was wet, he sold matches because the rain would have washed away his pictures if he had painted them. If it was fine, he was on his knees all day, making pictures in coloured chalks on the sidewalks, and doing them so quickly that often you would find he had painted up one side of a street and down the other almost before you'd had time to come round the corner.

On this particular day, which was fine but cold, he was painting. He was in the act of adding a picture of two bananas, an apple, and a head of Queen Elizabeth to a long string of others, when Mary Poppins walked up to him, tiptoeing so as to surprise him.

"Hey!" called Mary Poppins softly.

He went on putting brown stripes on a banana and brown curls on Queen Elizabeth's head.

"Ahem!" said Mary Poppins, with a ladylike cough.

He turned with a start and saw her.

"Mary!" he cried, and you could tell by the way he cried it that Mary Poppins was a very important person in his life.

Mary Poppins looked down at her feet and rubbed the toe of one shoe along the pavement two or three times. Then she smiled at the shoe in such a way that the shoe knew quite well that the smile wasn't meant for it.

"It's my Day, Bert," she said. "Didn't you remember?" Bert was the Match-Man's name — Herbert Alfred for Sundays.

"Of course I remembered, Mary," he said, "but —" and he stopped and looked sadly into his cap. It lay on the ground beside his last picture and there was tuppence in it. He picked it up and jingled the pennies.

"That all you got, Bert?" said Mary Poppins, and she said it so brightly you could hardly tell she was disappointed at all.

"That's the lot," he said. "Business is bad today. You'd think anybody'd be glad to pay to see that, wouldn't you?" And he nodded his head at Queen Elizabeth. "Well — that's how it is, Mary," he sighed. "Can't take you to tea today, I'm afraid."

Mary Poppins thought of the raspberry-jam-cakes they always had on her Day Out, and she was just going to sigh, when she saw the Match-Man's face. So, very cleverly, she turned the sigh into a smile — a good one with both ends turned up — and said, "That's all right, Bert. Don't you mind. I'd much rather not go to tea. A stodgy meal, I call it, really."

And that, when you think how very much she liked raspberry-jam-cakes, was rather nice of Mary Poppins.

The Match-Man apparently thought so, too, for he took her white-gloved hand in his and squeezed it hard. Then together they walked down the row of pictures.

"Now, *there's* one you've never seen before!" said the Match-Man proudly, pointing to a painting of a mountain covered with snow and its slopes simply littered with grasshoppers sitting on gigantic roses.

This time Mary Poppins could indulge in a sigh without hurting his feelings.

"Oh, Bert," she said, "that's a fair treat!" And by the way she said it she made him feel that by rights the picture should have been in the Royal Academy, which is a large room where people hang the pictures they have painted. Everybody comes to see them, and when they have looked at them for a very long time, everybody says to everybody else, "The idea — my dear!"

The next picture Mary Poppins and the Match-Man came to was even better. It was the country — all trees and grass and a little bit of blue sea in the distance, and something that looked like Margate in the background.

"My word!" said Mary Poppins admiringly, stooping so that she could see it better. "Why, Bert, whatever is the matter?"

For the Match-Man had caught hold of her other hand now, and was looking very excited.

"Mary," he said, "I got an idea! A real *idea*. Why don't we go there — right now — this very day? Both together, into the picture. Eh, Mary?" And still holding her hands, he drew her right out of the street, away from the iron railings and the lamp-posts, into the very middle of the picture. *Pff!* There they were, right inside it!

How green it was there and how quiet, and what soft crisp grass under their feet! They could hardly believe it was true, and yet here were green branches huskily rattling on their hats as they bent beneath them, and little coloured flowers curling round their shoes. They stared at each other, and each noticed that the other had changed. To Mary Poppins the Match-Man seemed to have bought himself an entirely new suit of clothes, for he was now wearing a bright green-and-red striped coat and white flannel trousers and, best of all, a new straw hat. He looked unusually clean, as though he had been polished.

"Why, Bert, you look fine!" she cried in an admiring voice.

Bert could not say anything for a moment, for his mouth had fallen open and he was staring at her with round eyes. Then he gulped and said, "Golly!"

That was all. But he said it in such a way and stared so steadily and so delightedly at her that she took a little mirror out of her bag and looked at herself in it.

She, too, she discovered, had changed. Round her shoulders hung a cloak of lovely artificial silk with watery patterns all over it, and the tickling feeling at the back of her neck came, the mirror told her, from a long curly feather that swept down from the brim of her hat. Her best shoes had disappeared, and in their place were others much finer and with large diamond buckles shining upon them. She was still wearing the white gloves and carrying the umbrella.

"My goodness," said Mary Poppins, "I *am* having a Day Out!"

So, still admiring themselves and each other, they moved on together through the little wood, till presently they came upon a little open space filled with sunlight. And there on a green table was Afternoon Tea!

A pile of raspberry-jam-cakes as high as Mary Poppins's waist stood in the centre, and beside it tea was boiling in a big brass urn. Best of all, there were two plates of whelks and two pins to pick them out with.

"Strike me pink!" said Mary Poppins. That was what she always said when she was pleased.

"Golly!" said the Match-Man. And that was *his* particular phrase.

"Won't you sit down, Moddom?" inquired a voice, and they turned to find a tall man in a black coat coming out of the wood with a table-napkin over his arm.

Mary Poppins, thoroughly surprised, sat down with a plop upon one of the little green chairs that stood round the table. The Match-Man, staring, collapsed onto another.

"I'm the Waiter, you know!" explained the man in the black coat.

"Oh! But I didn't see you in the picture," said Mary Poppins.

"Ah, I was behind the tree," explained the Waiter.

"Won't you sit down?" said Mary Poppins politely.

"Waiters never sit down, Moddom," said the man, but he seemed pleased at being asked.

"Your whelks, Mister!" he said, pushing a plate of them over to the Match-Man. "*And* your Pin!" He dusted the pin on his napkin and handed it to the Match-Man.

They began upon the afternoon tea, and the Waiter stood beside them to see they had everything they needed.

"We're having them after all," said Mary Poppins in a loud whisper, as she began on the heap of raspberry-jam-cakes.

"Golly!" agreed the Match-Man, helping himself to two of the largest.

"Tea?" said the Waiter, filling a large cup for each of them from the urn.

They drank it and had two cups more each, and then, for luck, they finished the pile of raspberry-jam-cakes. After that they got up and brushed the crumbs off.

"There is Nothing to Pay," said the Waiter, before they had time to ask for the bill. "It is a Pleasure. You will find the Merry-Go-Round just over there!" And he waved his hand to a little gap in the trees, where Mary Poppins and the Match-Man could see several wooden horses whirling round on a stand.

"That's funny," said she. "I don't remember seeing that in the picture, either."

"Ah," said the Match-Man, who hadn't remembered it himself, "it was in the Background, you see!"

The Merry-Go-Round was just slowing down as they approached it. They leapt upon it, Mary Poppins on a black horse and the Match-Man on a grey. And when the music started again and they began to move, they rode all the way to Yarmouth and back, because that was the place they both wanted most to see.

When they returned it was nearly dark and the Waiter was watching for them.

"I'm very sorry, Moddom and Mister," he said politely, "but we close at Seven. Rules, you know. May I show you the Way Out?"

They nodded as he flourished his table-napkin and walked on in front of them through the wood.

"It's a wonderful picture you've drawn this time, Bert," said Mary Poppins, putting her hand through the Match-Man's arm and drawing her cloak about her.

"Well, I did my best, Mary," said the Match-Man modestly. But you could see he was really very pleased with himself indeed.

Just then the Waiter stopped in front of them, beside a large white doorway that looked as though it were made of thick chalk lines.

"Here you are!" he said. "This is the Way Out."

"Good-bye, and thank you," said Mary Poppins, shaking his hand.

"Moddom, good-bye!" said the Waiter, bowing so low that his head knocked against his knees.

He nodded to the Match-Man, who cocked his head to one side and closed one eye at the Waiter, which was his way of bidding him farewell. Then Mary Poppins stepped through the white doorway and the Match-Man followed her.

And as they went, the feather dropped from her hat and the silk cloak from her shoulders and the diamonds from her shoes. The bright clothes of the Match-Man faded, and his straw hat turned into his old ragged cap again. Mary Poppins turned and looked at him, and she knew at once what had happened. Standing on the pavement, she gazed at him for a long minute, and then her glance explored the wood behind him for the Waiter. But the Waiter was nowhere to be seen. There was nobody in the picture. Nothing moved there. Even the Merry-Go-Round had disappeared. Only the still trees and the grass and the unmoving little patch of sea remained.

But Mary Poppins and the Match-Man smiled at one another. They knew, you see, what lay behind the trees. . . .

✦　✦　✦

When she came back from her Day Out, Jane and Michael came running to meet her.

"Where have you been?" they asked her.

"In Fairyland," said Mary Poppins.

"Did you see Cinderella?" said Jane.

"Huh, Cinderella? Not me," said Mary Poppins contemptuously. "Cinderella, indeed!"

"Or Robinson Crusoe?" asked Michael.

"Robinson Crusoe — pooh!" said Mary Poppins rudely.

"Then how could you have been there? It couldn't have been *our* Fairyland!"

Mary Poppins gave a superior sniff.

"Don't you know," she said pityingly, "that everybody's got a Fairyland of their own?"

And with another sniff she went upstairs to take off her white gloves and put the umbrella away.

✦ Stories of ✦
You and Me

The Monster

by Jean Van Leeuwen

Amanda is afraid of the scary night-monster upstairs. Can she and her father come up with a plan to make the monster go away? A reassuring story from Tales of Amanda Pig.

"**I** can't go upstairs," said Amanda. "There is a monster in the hall."

"That's dumb," said Oliver.

"Monsters are just pretend, Amanda," said Mother.

"Not this one," said Amanda.

"Show it to me," said Father.

Amanda pointed up the stairs.

"Hmm," said Father. "I always thought that was a clock."

"It is in the daytime," said Amanda. "At night it is a monster."

"I see what you mean," said Father. "There are its eyes."

"And its mouth," said Amanda. "And it has funny wings too."

"I don't think I want to go upstairs either," said Father.

"Oh, Father," said Amanda. "Grown-ups aren't scared of monsters."

"Not usually," said Father. "But this one is pretty scary."

"What can we do?" asked Amanda.

"Hmm," said Father. "I have an idea."

He got his flashlight and a cooking pot and two Halloween masks and his umbrella.

"Here is the plan," he said. "We will put on these masks. Then we will stamp upstairs. You will bang on the pot, and I will shine my flashlight in the monster's eyes. We are going to scare that monster."

"What is the umbrella for?" asked Amanda.

"Just in case," said Father.

Father and Amanda got ready.

"Watch out, Monster!" called Father. "We are coming up!"

Father and Amanda stamped upstairs.

Amanda banged on the pot.

Father shone his flashlight in the monster's eyes.

They stamped all the way down the hall to Amanda's room.

"Well, I guess we took care of that monster," said Father.

"When you were shining the light in the monster's eyes, it didn't look like a monster. It looked like a clock."

"Really?" said Father. "Then maybe there is no monster?"

"Maybe," said Amanda.

Father shone his flashlight at the monster again.

"That's a relief," said Father. "Now we can go to bed."

Father tucked Amanda in.

"Father," said Amanda. "What if I have to get up in the night and it is very dark and the clock looks like a monster again?"

"Hmm," said Father. "I know what. I will leave the masks and the pot and the flashlight and the umbrella by your bed."

"Just in case?" said Amanda.

"Just in case," said Father.

The Quilted Elephant and the Green Plush Dragon

by Alice Low

The quilted elephant, worn and tattered, was Roger's favorite stuffed animal . . . until he got a brand-new plush dragon for Christmas. Will these two rivals ever get along?

The quilted elephant and the green plush dragon both slept in Roger's bed. And they didn't like sharing it one bit.

The quilted elephant had always been Roger's favorite stuffed animal.

Roger's grandmother had made her from the one good corner of his worn-out baby quilt. Roger slept with the elephant every night.

Then, one Christmas, a brand-new green plush dragon sat under the tree. When Roger squeezed him, the dragon's fiery tongue darted out. And Roger made a loud, scary sound for him — R-R-ROARRR! The plush dragon liked that. It made him feel powerful. He was only a stuffed animal and couldn't make noises that people could hear. But the quilted elephant was jealous. Roger never made elephant noises for *her*.

74

Since then, Roger slept with them both, one arm around each. Before he fell asleep, Roger talked to the quilted elephant about all the things they had done together. When he did that, the plush dragon felt left out. But when Roger stroked the plush dragon, the quilted elephant felt unwanted and sad.

During the day, when Roger was at school, the elephant and the dragon never spoke to each other. The dragon tried once or twice, but the elephant was always asleep, or pretending to be.

Every afternoon, when Roger came home, he played with them both. But one afternoon, Roger didn't play with either of them. Instead, he started pulling things out of his dresser drawers.

"Something's happening!" said the dragon to the elephant. "Look! What's Roger up to?"

"Oh, my," said the elephant. "He's packing. That means he's going to sleep over."

"Will he take us?" asked the dragon.

"Well, I'm sure he'll take *me*. He always has. But there won't be room in his duffle for both of us."

"Then he'll take *me*, not *you*," said the dragon. "Your seams are split, and your stuffing is coming out."

"That's because he's played with me longer. I'm his oldest friend. He'll certainly take *me*."

Roger came back in. He picked up the plush dragon and hugged him. The dragon wanted to throw his paws around Roger and give him a dragon hug. But of course he couldn't.

Then Roger picked up the quilted elephant. The elephant wanted to curl her trunk around Roger and give him an elephant hug. But of course she couldn't.

"I don't know which one of you to choose," said Roger. "Maybe I can take you both.

"Uh-oh, there isn't room for either one of you. I know — maybe you'll both fit in the shopping bag with the present for Kevin.

"Oh, good, there *is* room, and for some toys, too."

"Oh, dear," said the dragon. "That box is going to poke a hole in my side."

"I don't mind being poked," said the elephant. "I'm full of holes already."

"It's awfully bumpy in here," said the dragon.

"It doesn't bother *me*," said the elephant. "I'm used to being tossed about."

"How far is he taking us?" asked the dragon.

"Only next door," said the elephant. "Now calm down."

✦　✦　✦

Kevin was waiting ouside. "Hi," he said. "You're late."

"The packing took longer than I thought," said Roger. "Here, I brought you a present."

"Wow! A boxcar for my trains! Thanks a lot. Let's go up to my room and play with them."

Roger followed Kevin upstairs and put both his bags in the closet. Then they hitched up the boxcar.

"It's dark in here," said the dragon. "I'm afraid of the dark, unless I'm with Roger. He's forgotten all about us now that he has Kevin."

"Stop complaining," said the elephant. "At least we have more room in here now. I'll just have a little snooze until Roger comes to get us."

But the dragon stayed awake, thinking. If only one of them

had fit in Roger's bag, which one would he have picked? And would Roger still love him if he *did* have a hole in his side?

He heard a noise — CLUNK-CLUNK-CLUNK. Then he heard a whirring sound. And then he heard Roger yell, "Let *me* do it."

WHIRR-WHIZ-ZOOM went the car.

"This is great," said Roger. "I wish I had one of these. Maybe we could trade."

"I'd never trade this one," said Kevin. "But I have a smaller car. Here, try it."

WHIRR-WHIZ-ZOOM went the smaller car. "It works fine," said Roger. "I love it. Okay, I'll trade. I'll go get my toys."

BUMP! The elephant woke up. The dragon fell on his side. They felt fingers poking them as Roger went through his bag.

"I'll trade for this," Roger said.

"One of the rotor blades is missing," said Kevin. "What else did you bring?"

"He can walk on slanted places," said Roger.

"Wham!" said Kevin. "He fell on his head."

Kevin made the wooden man fall down over and over again.

"So you'll trade?" asked Roger.

"I don't know," answered Kevin. "It's fun for a while, but then it gets boring. What else did you bring?"

"I didn't bring any other toys," said Roger.

"There's something else in that bag. I can tell," said Kevin.

The elephant and dragon lay there, frightened.

"These aren't toys," said Roger. "They're just my stuffed animals."

"Do they make noises if you squeeze them?" asked Kevin.

"No. But the dragon's tongue comes out. Watch!" Roger squeezed the dragon and went R-R-ROARRR!

"That's neat," said Kevin. He kept squeezing the dragon and running around with him, roaring. The dragon didn't like it. Kevin squeezed him too hard.

Then Kevin said, "This old elephant is losing its stuffing."

"That's because I play catch with her," said Roger.

They tossed the elephant back and forth. "This elephant is good for playing catch," said Kevin. The elephant didn't like the way Kevin threw her — fast and hard. But then Kevin made noises for her — TANTARATAROO! So *that* was how an elephant sounded!

Roger shouted "TANTARATAROO!" The elephant really liked that.

Suddenly, Kevin stopped playing. "Okay," he said. "I'll trade my car for the toys *and* the animals."

"You will?" asked Roger.

"Sure. Why not?" said Kevin.

Roger didn't answer. The elephant and the dragon waited, even more frightened.

"Because . . . ," said Roger. "Well . . . because I just found a hole in the dragon. And the elephant's losing more stuffing. I have to get Grandma to sew them both up tomorrow."

"My mom can do it," said Kevin. "Make up your mind tonight."

Roger and Kevin had supper and played downstairs. But upstairs, the elephant and the dragon waited and worried.

"We don't want to be Kevin's," said the dragon. "We love Roger."

"And he loves us," said the elephant. "But he loves that car, too."

"It would be awful to sleep in Kevin's bed," said the dragon.

"Awful!" said the elephant. "But more likely, he'd leave us on the floor all night."

Later, they watched Roger and Kevin getting ready for bed.

"So it's a trade?" asked Kevin.

"Yes," said Roger. "But just my toys. Not my animals."

"No deal," said Kevin. "Who cares about those animals, anyway?"

"*I* do," said Roger. And he picked them up and took them into bed.

"Don't worry," he whispered to them. "I'd never trade either of you. I couldn't sleep without you. Good night."

And he thought he heard two sighs — one rough and roary, and the other thin and trumpety.

Nora the Baby-Sitter

by Johanna Hurwitz

A funny story about a baby-sitting mix-up, from the book Busybody Nora.

Thursdays and Fridays were always fun. Thursday was Mommy's "day off." Mommy went out by herself, and Mrs. Michaels came upstairs with Russell and was the baby-sitter. On Friday, Mrs. Michaels also came upstairs with Russell, only on that day she left him and went out while Mommy was his baby-sitter. The apartment that Nora and Teddy lived in was a large one with more room for running about, which is why Russell came upstairs both days.

"Where are you going today?" asked Nora. She was watching Mommy put on her earrings. They were special "going-out" earrings that hung down, and she noticed that her mother had also put on lipstick.

"I'm going to get a haircut," said Mommy. "And then I'm going to meet my friend Elsa at the Metropolitan Museum for lunch."

Teddy was walking about the room wearing Mommy's good shoes. He watched her getting ready to go out, but he didn't cry. Ever since Mommy and Mrs. Michaels began to exchange baby-sitting he liked it when Mommy went out.

Their mother looked at the clock. "Nora, Mrs. Michaels will be here in five minutes. I have to stop at the bank, and I'm afraid there may be a long line and I'll be late. Will you be a big girl and take care of Teddy? Listen for the doorbell and ask who is it before you open the door."

Nora said yes, proudly. Sometimes Mommy left her alone for

a few minutes, when she went to the laundry room in the basement or to get the mail. It made Nora feel very grown-up, and Mommy said that it taught her responsibility. After all, soon she would finish kindergarten, and then she would be in first grade.

Teddy kissed Mommy good-bye.

Nora kissed Mommy good-bye on the lips, hoping some of the lipstick would come off on her.

Then Nora sat on the sofa and pretend read a book. It was *Madeline,* and she knew every word by heart. Just as she finished, the doorbell rang.

"It's Mrs. Michaels," called Teddy from his bedroom. He was building a block bridge and was afraid to lift his hand for fear that the entire structure would collapse.

"Who is it?" Nora asked from her side of the door.

"Russell and his mommy," called the voice from the other side.

Nora opened the door. There stood Mrs. Michaels. Instead of her usual slacks and ponytail, she was wearing a dress and her hair was pinned up on her head.

"Nora, sweetie, thank your mother for changing days with me. I've got to run. I have a doctor's appointment. See you at three o'clock, Russell," she said, kissing the top of her little boy's head.

And suddenly she was inside the elevator and gone.

Nora closed the door and locked it. "Russell," she said, in a voice full of wonder. "Today I am going to have lots of responsibility."

Russell smiled. He didn't speak yet, but Nora knew that he understood her when she spoke.

He started to run to the children's room, and Nora went after him. She was just in time to keep him from crashing into the bridge.

"This is the George Washington Bridge," said Teddy. "Don't you dare touch it."

"Here, Russell," said Nora, grabbing some unused blocks on the floor. "I'll help you build the Brooklyn Bridge." Diverted, Russell sat on the floor piling up blocks.

When the boys got tired of building, Nora offered to read to them. She pretend read *Madeline* three times and *Curious George* two times. She didn't miss a single word. Teddy would have corrected her if she had, because he also knew the stories by heart.

After reading so much, Nora was thirsty. She went to the refrigerator and took out a container of milk. Then she pushed a chair up close to the cupboard and took down the bottle of chocolate syrup. She made three glasses of chocolate milk, extra chocolaty. The three children drained their glasses.

"You're a good baby-sitter," said Teddy, as he rubbed off his chocolate moustache. "What's for lunch?"

There was a pause, but only for an instant. "Peanut-butter sandwiches."

"That's good," approved Teddy. The children always had peanut-butter sandwiches for lunch, whether it was Mommy or Mrs. Michaels baby-sitting.

Lunch was very good, even though Russell got peanut butter in his hair.

Then they all played house. Teddy was the daddy, and Nora was the mommy. Of course, Russell was the baby. Next they played ball, rolling several balls to each other, all at the same time. And then Nora decided it was time for Russell's nap. But Russell didn't seem at all tired. He kept running about, and he wouldn't lie down on either Teddy's or Nora's bed.

Nora had an idea. "Let's all lie down together on Mommy and Daddy's big bed."

The three children climbed up on the big bed. First they lay quietly. But then Teddy began to jump and bounce. And then Russell started jumping, too.

"Stop it this minute!" screamed Nora in her loudest voice. She tried to sound like Mommy.

"You heard what I said, and you are making me very angry."

Suddenly, even though she was the baby-sitter and it was time for Russell's nap, Nora couldn't help herself. She began to bounce on the bed, too

Next they all got down on the floor and did somersaults, bumping into one another. They crawled under the bed, where it was dark and spooky. And finally they all felt tired, and they lay down on the big bed again. This time they fell asleep.

Nora opened her eyes first. There stood Mommy, with a haircut and earrings and lipstick, and Mrs. Michaels in her dress with her hair pinned up. They were both crying and laughing at the same time.

"It's my fault," said Mrs. Michaels. "I forgot to remind you that we were switching days this week."

"No, no," said Mommy, tears running down her cheeks. "It's all my fault. I should have remembered."

"I shouldn't have left Russell and run off."

"How terrible that I just went off leaving Nora and Teddy here all alone. . . ."

"How awful. . . ."

Nora sat up in the bed. "Mommy," she said, beaming. "It was wonderful. No one took me to school, so I stayed home and *I* was the baby-sitter."

Mommy hugged her and hugged her.

Then Nora said, "Mommy, it was fun. But tomorrow I will need a day off."

Abuelo's House

by Kristine L. Franklin

*A gentle story about a young girl and
her special relationship with her
grandfather.*

" Abuelo, there's a dragon in the garden!"

When Claudia talks to her grandfather, she makes sure he sees her face.

"A BIG GREEN DRAGON!" Claudia speaks slowly, and sometimes she says things twice. "REALLY BIG, Abuelo. *Grande.*"

It helps if she uses her hands to show Abuelo what she means. "BIG! Come out and see."

"*¿Un dragón?*" says Abuelo. "We had better take care of it right now."

Abuelo can't hear. The inside part of his ears that used to hear birds and music and talking doesn't work anymore. When Claudia plugs her ears tight, she still hears noises. All Abuelo hears is quiet.

87

Claudia helps Abuelo squirt the dragon with the hose before it burns up the tomatoes. If she needs to get Abuelo's attention, she pats his arm. Screaming and yelling don't help one bit.

"Over there! Another dragon! See the smoke?" The pretend dragon hisses and disappears when Abuelo squirts it.

"Do you see any more?" asks Abuelo.

"No." Claudia shakes her head. She takes Abuelo's rough old hand, and they go inside. Abuelo knows all about dragons. He knows all about gardens, too.

Claudia spends part of each summer at Abuelo's house. Every summer they plant a vegetable garden with peas and beans and corn and tomatoes. They water the garden and pull all the weeds. They make sure the dragons stay away. They ride bikes, too, every day, when they aren't busy tending the garden. On rainy days Claudia helps Abuelo with his work.

Abuelo is an artist. He has a studio in his house. There are drawings and paintings and pencils and more paints than Claudia has ever seen. She helps by putting the little tubes of paint in piles.

"What is this color called, Abuelo?"

"Little-girl-with-brown-eyes brown," says Abuelo.

"What are you painting now, Abuelo?" When Claudia asks "what?" it is like a shrug.

"*Una sorpresa,*" says Abuelo.

"A surprise? For me? Tell me, Abuelo!" Claudia hops up and down. She waves her hands. She points to the painting. Then she points to herself. "Is it for me?" Abuelo pretends not to notice. His eyes crinkle up. He smiles. But he does not tell.

"Please tell me the surprise, Abuelo, PLEASE!"

Abuelo shakes his head. Abuelo can be very stubborn.

When Claudia eats lunch at Abuelo's house, she has to clean

her plate. Sometimes she doesn't like the food. She is glad Abuelo can't hear her complain. "These tortillas are too dry," says Claudia.

"Eat the tortillas," says Abuelo with a frown. Abuelo knows all about children.

"Who is the special painting for?" Claudia asks. Abuelo can't hear her pouty voice. She tears the tortillas into little pieces. She puts the tortilla pieces in straight rows across her plate.

"No more questions about the painting," says Abuelo sternly. "Eat!"

"I [stomp] WANT [stomp] TO [stomp] KNOW [stomp] THE [stomp] SURPRISE [stomp] RIGHT [stomp] NOW!" Claudia yells.

Abuelo feels the floor shake. "Stop making all that noise," he scolds.

In the evening, Claudia and Abuelo watch Abuelo's special TV. Claudia listens, and Abuelo watches the little words at the bottom of the picture. They laugh at all the jokes together. Once, when Abuelo laughs especially hard, Claudia pats his arm. "Who is that secret painting for, Abuelo?" He laughs even harder. Little tears squeeze out of his eyes.

"You're snoopy," says Abuelo.

"You're very stubborn, Abuelo."

A light flashes in the room. Abuelo's telephone is ringing.

FLASH! FLASH! Abuelo picks up the phone. He puts it on a little machine that looks like a typewriter. Claudia calls it the Abuelo-phone. She has an Abuelo-phone at her house so she can call Abuelo and Abuelo can call her. Abuelo types H-E-L-L-O.

"Hi, Papa," the Abuelo-phone types back. It is Claudia's mother. The Abuelo-phone clicks and beeps. Abuelo and Claudia's mother type back and forth.

Then Abuelo types G-O-O-D-B-Y-E and hangs up the phone.

"Your mother will be here next Sunday to pick you up," he says. Claudia is very quiet. "Don't be sad, *preciosa*," says Abuelo. "You will come again next summer."

Claudia shows Abuelo OK and nods. This is the only part of summer she doesn't like.

"Let's go out to the studio," Abuelo says. "I have something special to show you."

Inside the studio Abuelo shows Claudia the secret painting. It is covered with a cloth, but Claudia isn't curious anymore. "Don't you want to see your surprise?" asks Abuelo.

"OK," says Claudia. It wouldn't be nice to hurt Abuelo's feelings. Claudia lifts the cloth.

The painting is Claudia! It's Claudia and Abuelo and the garden and the red tomatoes and the hot yellow sun and the blue sky and green green beans and the tall corn with fuzzy silk sticking out at the tops.

"Oh, Abuelo, it's the best surprise I've ever had, the *very* best!" Claudia jumps into Abuelo's arms and squeezes him around the neck. "I love you, Abuelito." Abuelo understands hugs.

He carries Claudia to the window. They look out at the wonderful garden. With a twinkle in his eyes, Abuelo says, "I see a puff of smoke out there."

He puts Claudia down and takes her hand. They go outside together. Claudia and Abuelo have some dragons to squirt before the summer ends.

Paul

by Louis Sachar

Have you ever really wanted to do something, but knew you shouldn't? Paul sure has! Read all about it in this hilarious tale from Sideways Stories from Wayside School.

Paul had the best seat in Mrs. Jewls's class. He sat in the back of the room. It was the seat that was the farthest away from Mrs. Jewls.

Mrs. Jewls was teaching the class about fractions. She drew a picture of a pie on the blackboard. She cut the pie into eight pieces. She explained that each piece was one eighth of the pie.

Paul never paid attention. He didn't see the picture of the pie. He didn't see anything.

Well, he did see one thing.

Actually, he saw two things.

He saw Leslie's two pigtails.

Leslie sat in front of Paul. She had two long, brown pigtails that reached all the way down to her waist.

Paul saw those pigtails, and a terrible urge came over him. He wanted to pull a pigtail. He wanted to wrap his fist around it, feel the hair between his fingers, and just yank.

He thought it would also be fun to tie the pigtails together, or better yet, tie them to her chair. But most of all, he just wanted to pull one.

Slowly he reached for the one on the right. "NO! What am I doing?" he thought. "I'll only get into trouble."

Paul had it made. He sat in the back of the room. He paid no attention to anyone, and nobody paid any attention to him. But if he pulled a pigtail, it would be all over. Leslie would tell on him, and he'd become the center of attention.

He sighed and slowly withdrew his arm.

But Paul couldn't ignore those pigtails. There they were, dangling right in front of him, just begging to be pulled. He could close his eyes, but he couldn't make the pigtails disappear. He could still smell them. And hear them. He could almost taste them.

"Maybe just a little tug," he thought. "No, none."

There they hung, easily within his reach.

"Well let them just hang there!" thought Paul.

It would be foolish to pull one, no matter how tempting they were. None of the other children in the class pulled pigtails; why should he? Of course, none of the other children sat behind Leslie, either.

It was just a simple matter of being able to think clearly. That was all. Paul thought it over and decided not to pull one. It was as simple as that.

Suddenly his arm shot forward. He grabbed Leslie's right pigtail and yanked.

"Yaaaaaahhhhhhhhhhh!" screamed Leslie.

Everybody looked at her.

"Paul pulled my pigtail," she said.

They all looked at Paul.

"I — I couldn't help it," said Paul.

"You'd better learn to help it," said Mrs. Jewls. She wrote Paul's name on the blackboard under the word DISCIPLINE. "Tell Leslie you're sorry."

"I'm sorry, Leslie," said Paul.

"Hmmmph," said Leslie.

Paul felt horrible. Never again would he pull another pigtail! Except, there was one problem. He still wasn't satisfied. He had pulled the right one, but that wasn't enough. He wanted to pull the left one, too. It was as if he heard a little voice coming from the pigtail saying, "Pull me, Paul. Pull me."

"I can't," Paul answered. "My name's already on the blackboard under the word DISCIPLINE."

"Big deal," said the pigtail. "Pull me."

"No way," said Paul. "Never again."

"Aw, come on, Paul, just a little tug," urged the pigtail. "What harm could it do?"

"Lots of harm," said Paul. "Leslie will scream, and I'll get in trouble again."

"Boy, that's not fair," whined the pigtail. "You pulled the right one. Now it's my turn."

"I know, but I can't," said Paul.

"Sure you can," said the pigtail. "Just grab me and yank."

"No," said Paul. "It's not right."

"Sure it is, Paul," said the pigtail. "Pigtails are meant to be pulled. That's what we're here for."

"Tell that to Leslie," said Paul.

"Leslie won't mind," said the pigtail. "I promise."

"I bet," said Paul. "Just like she didn't mind the last time."

"You just didn't pull hard enough," said the pigtail. "Leslie likes us pulled real hard."

"Really?" asked Paul.

"Cross my heart," said the pigtail. "The harder, the better."

"Okay," said Paul, "but if you're lying . . ."

"I promise," said the pigtail.

Paul grabbed the left pigtail. It felt good in his hand. He pulled as hard as he could.

"Yaaaaaaaaaahhhhhhhhhhhhhhhhhhhhhh!!!" screamed Leslie.

Mrs. Jewls asked, "Paul, did you pull Leslie's pigtail again?"

"No," said Paul. "I pulled the other one."

All the children laughed.

"Are you trying to be funny?" asked Mrs. Jewls.

"No," said Paul. "I was trying to be fair. I couldn't pull one and not the other."

The children laughed again.

"Pigtails are meant to be pulled," Paul concluded.

Mrs. Jewls put a check next to Paul's name on the blackboard under the word DISCIPLINE.

But at last Paul was satisfied. True, his name was on the blackboard with a check next to it, but that really didn't matter. All he had to do was stay out of trouble the rest of the day, and his name would be erased. It's easy to stay out of trouble when you have the best seat in the class.

In fact, Paul could do this every day. He could pull Leslie's pigtails twice, and then stay out of trouble the rest of the day. There was nothing Leslie could do about it.

Suddenly, out of nowhere, Leslie screamed, "Yaaaahhhhh-hhh!"

Mrs. Jewls circled Paul's name and sent him home early on the kindergarten bus. Nobody would believe that he hadn't pulled Leslie's pigtail again.

Maria's Invisible Cat

by Barbara Giles

Maria's cat is just make-believe . . . or is it?

Maria thought a lot about having her own cat. Should she have a black cat, a tabby cat, a white cat?

"What color cat do you like best, Dad?"

"I've told you not to ask for a cat," said her mother.

"I'm not asking," said Maria. "What color, Dad?"

"Black, I suppose. But Mom doesn't want a cat."

"My cat is black, with a white tip to his tail," said Maria. "I can't think what to call him."

"Call him Nix," said Dad. "That means 'nothing.' No-cat. Remember what Mom said."

Maria liked the name. "Nix is very little," she said. "Not much bigger than nothing. And he doesn't eat much."

At kindergarten, Maria painted a black kitten with a white tip to his tail.

"His name's Nix," she said to her teacher. "Please write it for me."

When her mother saw the painting she said, "You can't have a cat."

"I know," said Maria, "but please put up the picture for me."

Her mother stuck it up on the wall with tape.

After lunch, Maria found an old saucer. "Can I have this for Nixie?"

"There's no milk for No-cat," said her mother.

"I know, I know," said Maria. "Can I have this box for his bed? Can I put it on the back porch? Could he have this old sweater to sleep on?"

Her mother sighed.

Next morning, Maria opened the back door. "Are you there, Nix? Come on, I've brought you some milk. Drink up, Nixie, so you'll grow big."

"You're a silly," said her mom. "All that carrying on about a cat that isn't there! Now come and get ready for kindergarten."

"Okay. Good-bye, Nixie. I'll see you when I get home."

When Dad came home that night she said, "What *do* you think Nix was up to today? He was trying to get in the cat-door."

"Don't you unfasten that door," said Mom, "or we'll have some stray in before you can sneeze. I meant it. No cats."

"Okay," said Maria. "He likes it outside."

Each day, Maria took food and milk out to Nix. At least, that's what she said, but the saucer was just as empty when she carried it out, very carefully so as not to spill any milk, as when she brought it back inside.

She shook out his bed and washed his saucer, and she talked to him a lot. She played with him, rolling a little pink ball. When the next-door neighbors' dog got in, she said, "Quickly, Nix. Up the plum tree. He can't get you there."

She even took a photograph of him in the plum tree. "You can't see him for the blossom," she said, "but there's the tip of his tail."

After a while her parents got quite used to all this. Some nights her dad would say, "Have you fed your cat?" Or he'd ask where Nix was hiding himself.

Her mother said nothing, except that the empty box by the door looked untidy.

"He's no trouble at all, your little Nix," said Dad. "He doesn't scratch up the garden or chase the birds. Nobody would know we had a cat at all."

"We *don't*," said Mom. "And that's the way it's going to stay. Maria's is quite the best kind of cat. Invisible."

One night there was a storm that blew the rain right up to the back door. Maria brought the box inside.

"Nixie has to come in, or he'll get wet," she said.

"Well, just this once," said Dad with a wink.

Next day, the sun was shining after the rain, and Maria felt as if something good was going to happen.

During breakfast she heard a small sound outside, and she opened the door. On the mat was a small black kitten.

"Nix," said Maria. "Nixie. So here you are."

The little cat meowed softly.

"I didn't keep asking, did I?" said Maria. "But he's come. I *can* keep him, can't I, Dad?"

"Perhaps he isn't here to stay. He may live somewhere nearby," said her father. "I don't know what Mom will say, but I'll talk to her."

"See, here's his little white-tipped tail — just like I drew him," said Maria. "Are you hungry, Nixie?"

She filled his saucer with real milk, and Nixie lapped it up quickly.

"Look at his little pink tongue. And he's got a white patch on his back leg. I didn't know about that." She stroked him. "Nixie, Nixie, you *are* hungry. Nice puss. I'll fetch your box."

The cat jumped into the box, purring, as if he belonged there. He was sleepy now. "Will you tell Mom he's here, in his box, Dad? Tell her I won't let him inside. He'll be *almost* invisible. He will, really. *Please,* Dad."

Later she heard her parents talking. Nothing was said about sending Nix away. No one came looking for a small black cat.

Each day Maria fed Nix on the back porch. She washed his saucer and shook out the sweater from his box.

Nix was growing. He was quick and full of play. But he stayed outside. Mom ignored him when she came out. Nix was very quiet then, and crept into his box. He seemed to know she didn't like cats.

One Saturday morning, Maria and her father drove to the city to buy a special birthday present for Mom.

While they were out, Joe from next door raced in carrying Nix.

"Your little cat, Mrs. Drew," he said sadly. "He's had an accident. Broken his leg, I'd say. Must have been hit by a car."

"Poor little fellow," said Maria's mom. "We must get him to the vet quickly. But the car isn't here."

"I'll take you," said Joe.

So they went to the vet in Joe's big red truck.

The vet soon had Nix's broken leg in a cast. "He is all right, but for the leg," he said. "Keep him quiet if you can."

When they got home, Mrs. Drew made a bed for Nix in her old Chinese sewing basket and put it on the porch. Nix lay quietly and stared up at her with his green eyes.

She went into the house.

Then she came out again.

"It's a bit cold out here for a hurt cat," she said, and she carried the basket into the kitchen and put it down near Maria's cat painting.

She sat down on the floor beside Nix and stroked his head.

"You're a good little cat, Nixie," she said. "How could I send you away?"

She was still sitting there, talking to Nix, when Maria and her father came home.

"He'll be all right," she said, getting up quickly. "Just a broken leg. Fetch him a saucer of milk, Maria. And unhook the cat-door, so he can let himself in and out. He's a smart little cat; he'll soon understand how it works."

"He's smart, but no longer invisible," said Dad with a smile at Maria.

Nix drank a little milk and tried walking on three legs. He was awkward at first, and timid, but soon he was sniffing his way around the kitchen as if he belonged there.

"This is home, Nix," whispered Maria, "and you're here to stay."

"By the way, Maria," said Mom. "You could throw away that beat-up box of his. He'll be much more comfortable in this basket."

So it was lucky that Maria's birthday present for Mom was a special wooden box, with lots of compartments and tiny drawers with brass handles, to keep her sewing things in.

A Curve in the River

by Ann Cameron

When Julian puts a message in a bottle and drops it in the river, he hopes it will travel clear across the world. . . . A special story about friendship from the book More Stories Julian Tells.

This is something I learned in school: The whole body is mostly water.

We think we're solid, but we're not. You can tell sometimes from your blood and tears and stuff that what you're like inside isn't what you're like outside, but usually you'd never know.

Also, the whole earth is mostly water — three quarters ocean. The continents are just little stopping places. And using water — streams and rivers and oceans — anybody could put a message in a bottle and send it all the way around the world.

That was my secret project.

I had a bottle with a cork. I had paper and a ballpoint pen. I wrote a message: *Whoever finds this bottle, please write or call me and tell me where you found it.*

I put down my address and phone number. Then I corked the bottle and carried it down to the river.

105

I threw the bottle as far out as I could. It splashed, bobbed up, and floated. I watched it go out of sight.

I kept thinking about my secret project.

Maybe my bottle was on the way to Hawaii.

Maybe it was on the way to France.

Maybe it was on the way to China.

Maybe I would write letters to the person who found it, and we would become friends. I would go visit the person where he or she lived.

I could see myself in Rio de Janeiro, dancing in the streets.

I could see myself in India, riding on an elephant.

I could see myself in Africa, taming wild lions.

A week went by.

I wondered how long I'd have to wait before I heard from the person who got my bottle. It might be months.

Maybe my bottle would go to the North Pole and be found stuck in the ice by Eskimo hunters. Then I realized it might lie in the ice for years before it was found. Somebody might phone or write me, and I would even have forgotten about my bottle.

I decided I should write a note to myself and hide it in my desk, where I would find it when I grew up, so I could remind myself about the bottle then.

Dear Old Julian, I wrote. *Remember the bottle you threw in the river?* And then I put down the day and the year that I threw it in.

I had just finished hiding this message in the back of my desk when the phone rang.

It was Gloria.

"Julian, I have some news!" she said.

"Oh, really?" I said. Nothing could be important news that wasn't about my bottle.

"Julian," Gloria said, "it's about your bottle with the message — I found it!" She sounded happy. I wasn't. My bottle was supposed to travel around the world.

"Julian?" Gloria said.

I didn't answer.

All that water to travel! All those countries to see! The whole world full of strangers! And where did my stupid bottle go? To Gloria's house!

"Julian?" Gloria said. "Are you still there?"

I couldn't talk. I was too disgusted. I hung up.

◆   ◆   ◆

Gloria came looking for me.

"Tell her I'm not here," I said to Huey.

Huey went to the door. "Julian says he's not here," Huey said.

"Oh," Gloria said. She went away.

In a couple of days my father started noticing.

"I haven't seen Gloria lately," he said.

"I don't want to see her," I said.

"Why?" my father said.

"Because."

Then I decided to tell my father about the bottle and how Gloria found it. It didn't matter anymore to keep it a secret. The secret was over.

"That's too bad," my father said. "But it's not Gloria's fault."

"She found the bottle," I said. "She must be laughing at me for trying such a stupid idea."

"It's not a stupid idea," my father said. "You just had bad luck. You know what your problem is? It's the curve in the river. Your bottle got stuck on that curve, and it didn't have a chance."

I felt a little better. I went to see Gloria.

"I wanted to give you your bottle back," Gloria said. Then she added, "I thought it was a great idea, sending a message in a bottle."

"Well, it's a good idea, but it's a no-good idea because of the curve in the river. The bottle couldn't get around it," I explained.

"I guess it couldn't," Gloria said.

"Julian," my father said, "I have to make a long trip in the truck Saturday. I have to pick up some car parts. I'm going to go past the big bridge down the river. Would you like to ride along?"

I said I would.

"You know," my father said, "there's something we could do. We could walk out on the bridge. And if you wanted, you could send a new message. Your bottle would have a good chance from there. It's past the curve in the river."

I thought about it. I decided to do it. And I told my father.

"You know," he said, "if you don't mind my advice — put something special about yourself in the bottle, for the person who finds it."

"Why?" I asked.

"It'll give the wind and the water something special to carry. If you send something you care about, it might bring you luck."

I was working on my new message. And then I thought about Huey and Gloria. I thought how they might want to send bottles, too. It didn't seem so important anymore that I be the only one to do it.

And that's what we did. We all got new bottles, and we put something special in each one. We each made a picture of ourselves for our bottle.

And in his, Huey put his favorite joke:
Where does a hamburger go on New Year's Eve?
To a meat ball.

In hers, Gloria put instructions on doing a cartwheel.

In mine, I wrote instructions for taking care of rabbits.

We added our addresses and phone numbers and pushed in the corks tightly. We were ready for Saturday.

The bridge was long and silver and sparkled in the sun. It was so big that it looked like giants must have made it, that human be-

ings never could have. But human beings did.

My father parked below the bridge. "From here we have to walk," he said.

We got out of the truck, which always smells a little bit of dust, but mostly of the raisins Dad keeps on the dashboard.

We walked in the outside walkers' lane to the middle of the river. Cars whizzed past. We each had our bottle in a backpack.

The bridge swayed a little. We could feel it vibrate. My father held Gloria's and Huey's hands. I held Gloria's other hand.

"It's scary, but it's safe," my father said.

We held on to the bridge railing and looked over the side. The green water slid under us very fast. For a minute it seemed like the bridge was moving and the water was standing still.

We unpacked our bottles.

"Don't just throw them over the side," my father said. "Make some wishes. Sending messages around the world is a big thing to do. Anytime you do a big thing, it's good to make wishes."

We did.

I don't know what Huey or Gloria wished. I wished our bottles would sail along together. I wished they wouldn't get trapped in seaweed or ice, or hit rocks. I wished we'd make new friends on the other side of the world. I wished we'd go to meet them someday.

"Ready?" my father said.

Together we threw our bottles over the side. They made a tiny splash. They looked very small, but we could see them starting toward the ocean.

They were like Columbus's ships. I hoped they'd stay together a long, long time.

The Radish Cure

by Betty MacDonald

Who can help Patsy's mother get her stubborn daughter to take a much-needed bath? Why, Mrs. Piggle-Wiggle, of course! A very funny story from the book Mrs. Piggle-Wiggle, *the first in a series about this wise heroine.*

Up to the time of this story Patsy was just an everyday little girl. Sometimes she was good and sometimes she was naughty but usually she did what her mother told her without too much fuss. BUT ONE MORNING Patsy's mother filled the bathtub with nice warm water and called to Patsy to come and take her bath. Patsy came into the bathroom but when she saw the nice warm tub of water she began to scream and yell and kick and howl like a wild animal.

Naturally her mother was quite surprised to see her little girl acting so peculiarly but she didn't say anything, just took off Patsy's bathrobe and said, "Now, Patsy, stop all this nonsense and hop into the tub."

Patsy gave a piercing shriek and ran from the bathroom stark naked and yelling, "I won't take a bath! I won't ever take a

bath! I hate baths! I HATE BATHS! I haaaaaaaaaaaaaaate baaaaaaaaaaaaths!"

Patsy's mother let the water out of the tub and went downstairs to telephone her friends and find out if their children had ever behaved in this unusual fashion; if it was catching and what to do about it.

First she called Mrs. Brown. She said, "Hello, Mrs. Brown. This is Patsy's mother and I am having such a time this morning. Patsy simply will not take a bath. Pardon me, just a minute, Mrs. Brown."

She put down the telephone receiver and went over to Patsy, who was standing in the kitchen doorway listening to the telephone conversation and feeling very important.

Patsy said, "What did Mrs. Brown say to do with me, Mother?"

Patsy's mother said, "She hasn't told me yet but while I am finding out you had better march right upstairs and get dressed and then you can pick up that messy, sticky pasting work you left all over your room last night. Don't come downstairs until every single thing is put away."

Patsy's mother picked up the telephone and Mrs. Brown said, "I'm sorry but I can't offer any suggestions because our little Prunella just adores to bathe. Perhaps Mrs. Grotto could help you."

So Patsy's mother called Mrs. Grotto. She said, "Hello, Mrs. Grotto, I just called to ask if you could help me with Patsy. She won't take a bath and I am at my wits' end."

Mrs. Grotto said, "Well, frankly, I don't know what to suggest because our little Paraphernalia simply worships her bath. Of course, Paraphernalia is quite a remarkable child anyway. Why, Thursday afternoon she said —"

"Yes, yes, I know," said Patsy's mother quickly. "Good-bye, Mrs. Grotto, thank you anyway."

Then Patsy's mother called Mrs. Broomrack. "Good morning, Mrs. Broomrack," she said a little too brightly. "I wonder if you would do me a favor?"

"Why, of course, dear, of course!" said Mrs. Broomrack.

"Well," said Patsy's mother, "this morning for the first time in her life, our little Patsy won't take a bath. The very idea seems to make her hysterical and I don't know what to do."

Mrs. Broomrack said, "Why, you poor dear, all alone in that big house with that unmanageable child. Personally, I don't know what to say because our little Cormorant looks forward so to taking a bath. Bathing is his favorite pastime. In fact, sometimes we can't get him out of the tub."

"Why don't you let him stay in, then?" said Patsy's mother.

"Because he might drown!" squealed Mrs. Broomrack.

"Well . . . ," said Patsy's mother, as she hung up the phone.

By this time she was feeling rather depressed because it seemed that bathing was the most popular indoor sport with every child in town but her own dirty little girl.

In desperation she decided to call Mrs. Piggle-Wiggle. "She should know about children," thought Patsy's mother. "She certainly has her house crawling with them, day and night."

It certainly was fortunate for Patsy's mother that she thought of Mrs. Piggle-Wiggle, because although Mrs. Piggle-Wiggle has no children of her own and lives in an upside-down house, she understands children better than anybody in the whole world. She is always ready to stop whatever she is doing and have a tea party. She is glad to have children dig worms in her petunia bed. She has a large trunk full of scraps for doll clothes and another trunk full of valuable rocks with gold in them. She is delighted to have children pick up and look at all the little things which she keeps on her tables and when Hubert Prentiss dropped the glass ball that snowed on the children when you shook it, she said, "Heavens, Hubert, don't cry. I'm so glad this happened. For years and years I have wanted to know what was in that glass ball." Mrs. Piggle-Wiggle takes it for granted that you will want to try on her shoes and go wiggling around on high heels.

Which is probably why she was not at all surprised when Patsy's mother told her about the bath. "I suppose we all come to it sooner or later," she said. "Well, from my experience I would say that the Radish Cure is probably the quickest and most lasting."

"The radish cure?" said Patsy's mother.

"Yes," said Mrs. Piggle-Wiggle. "The Radish Cure is just

what Patsy needs. All you have to do is buy one package of radish seeds. The small red round ones are the best, and don't get that long white icicle type. Then, let Patsy strictly alone, as far as washing is concerned, for several weeks. When she has about half an inch of rich black dirt all over her and after she is asleep at night, scatter radish seeds on her arms and head. Press them in gently and then just wait. I don't think you will have to water them because we are in the rainy season now and she probably will go outdoors now and then. When the little radish plants have three leaves you may begin pulling the largest ones.

"Oh, yes, Patsy will probably look quite horrible before the Radish Cure is over, so if you find that she is scaring too many people or her father objects to having her around, let me know and I will be glad to take her over here. You see, all of my visitors are children and dirt doesn't frighten them."

Patsy's mother thanked Mrs. Piggle-Wiggle very, very much for her kind advice and then called up Patsy's father and told him to be sure and bring home a package of radish seeds. Early Red Globe, she thought they were called.

The next morning she didn't say one single word to Patsy about a bath and so Patsy was sweet and didn't act like a wild animal. The next day was the same and so was the next and the next.

When Sunday came Patsy was a rather dark blackish gray color so her mother suggested that she stay home from Sunday School.

Patsy's father, who by this time had been told of the Radish Cure, didn't say anything to Patsy about washing but he winced whenever he looked at her.

By the end of the third week they had to keep Patsy indoors all of the time because one morning she skipped out to get the mail and the postman, on seeing her straggly, uncombed, dust-caked hair and the rapidly forming layer of topsoil on her face, neck, and arms, gave a terrified yell and fell down the front steps.

Patsy seemed quite happy though. Of course, it was getting hard to tell how she felt as her face was so caked with dirt that she couldn't smile and she talked "oike is — I am Atsy and I on't ake a ath." She also had to take little teeny bites of food because she couldn't open her mouth more than a crack.

Naturally her father and mother had to stop having any friends in to visit except in the evening when Patsy was in bed and even then they were not at all comfortable for fear Patsy would wake up and call, "Ing e a ink of ater, Addy!" (Really, "Bring me a drink of water, Daddy!")

At last, however, the day came when Patsy was ready to plant. That night when she was asleep her mother and father tiptoed into her room and very gently pressed radish seeds into her forehead, her arms, and the backs of her hands. When they had finished and were standing by her bed gazing fondly at their handiwork, Patsy's father said, "Repulsive little thing!"

Patsy's mother said, "Why, George, that's a terrible thing to say of your own child!"

"My little girl is buried so deep in that dirt that I can't even remember what she looks like," said Patsy's father, and he stamped down the stairs.

The Radish Cure is certainly hard on the parents.

Quite a few days after that Patsy awoke one morning and there on the back of her hand, in fact on the backs of both hands and on her arms and on her FOREHEAD, were GREEN LEAVES! Patsy tried to brush them off but they just bent over and sprang right up again.

She jumped out of bed and ran down the stairs to the dining

room, where her mother and father were eating breakfast. "Ook, ook, at y ands!" she squeaked.

Her father said, "Behold the bloom of youth," and her mother said, "George!" then jumped up briskly, went over to Patsy, took a firm hold of one of the plants on her forehead and gave it a quick jerk. Patsy squealed and her mother showed her the little red radish she had pulled. Patsy tried to pull one out of her arm, but her hands were so caked with dirt that they couldn't grasp the little leaves so her mother had to pull them.

When they had finished one hand and part of the left arm, Patsy suddenly said, "Other, I ant a ath!"

"What did you say?" asked her mother, busily pulling the radishes and putting them in neat little piles on the dining room table.

"I oowant a b . . . b . . . ath!" said Patsy so plainly that it cracked the mud on her left cheek.

Patsy's mother said, "I think it had better be a shower," and without another word she went in and turned on the warm water.

Patsy was in the shower all that day — she used up two whole bars of soap and she didn't even come out for lunch but when her father came home for dinner, there she was, waiting for him at the door; clean, sweet and smiling, and in her hand she had a plate of little red radishes.

The Fish That Got Left in the Tide Pool

by Margaret Wise Brown

A seashore surprise awaits a young boy in this gentle story by the author of such childhood classics as Goodnight Moon *and* The Runaway Bunny.

There was a tide pool left in the rocks when the tide went out, a clear bright pool of water, clear as glass to see through, with green plants growing on its rocky bottom like a wavy, watery, green forest. It looked like a small ocean the size of a puddle in the rocky hollow that held it. Little plants and animals lived in it just as they did under the ocean, where only the fishes saw them. And when the wind blew, it made small waves on top of the tide pool just as it did on the top of the ocean.

Tommy found the tide pool one day when he was scrambling and climbing around the big rocks. Tommy lived not very far off from the big rocks, so that every day when the tide went out, he ran over to see what the ocean had left in his tide pool.

There were barnacles there, little soft squashy animals that lived in hard scratchy shells. They were always there. And there were blue mussels clinging to the sides of the pool, and one pale yellow periwinkle. But there was something else. Things most wonderful. Yellow and Red and Orange and Pink. They were sea anemones, rosy-fingered animals that opened up like flowers and then closed, looking like small orange potatoes clinging to the rocks. They ate things, too. If you touched one very lightly with a piece of seaweed, it would open up; its long rosy white streamers would come out like flower petals and grab the baby sand worms and the black and yellow wiggle-bugs that swam past it. Then the streamers would fold up again and carry the food back into the anemone's mouth.

But this day, that was Tuesday, when Tommy came to his tide pool, there was Something That Had Never Been There Before. It was alive. It was a fish. Tommy leaned way out over the edge of the pool and watched it. It swam in and out among the wavy green plants; and then it rested under a large flat leaf of floating seaweed.

"What a poky little fish you must have been to have got left way up here on the rocks when the tide went out! A poky little fish."

Tommy watched it for a long time.

But Tommy was not the only one watching the fish. He heard the "*Crack-crack-cawk*" of a seagull above him; and looking up, he saw a great white bird with gray wings flying in the air, sliding sideways down the wind. A hungry seagull.

"Old seagull," said Tommy, "look what the tide has left in my tide pool. It's a poky fish. Did you ever see a fish get left in a tide pool when the tide went out?"

But the seagull only screamed his seagull noise and wheeled in the air above Tommy's head, swooping down always nearer to the tide pool and to Tommy's little fish.

Tommy lay on his tummy on the rocks in the afternoon sun

and wiggled his fingers in the pool to make the fish dart around in the green forest that the seaweed made. This was even more fun than when the tide left a scuttling crab in his pool. The crab just scuttled sideways when it was poked, and tried to hide among the small rocks at one end of the pool and pretend that it was another rock. But the little fish swam round and round. And the seagull kept slowly flying, gray and white in the sky above.

All this time the tide was coming in. Tommy could hear it splashing louder on the rocks as it came nearer. Pretty soon it would cover the rocks, tide pool and all. Then the little fish would swim back into the ocean. Tommy wondered if the fish would ever get sleepy again and stay in his tide pool. It was such a pretty little green and blue fish, with its spiky fins. But the tide was roaring in, icy green over the sand and rocks, and the sun was going down the sky toward the water. Tommy thought he had better go back to his house and see his mother.

"Good-bye, Poky Fish," said Tommy. "Good-bye, Noisy Sea-gull."

And he started for home across the rocks. But no sooner had he turned his back than he heard a terrible fluttering, and he turned in time to see the seagull swoop down toward his fish. "HI!" Tommy hollered. Just in time. The seagull brushed past the water of the tide pool and up in the air again. But it had not caught his fish.

Tommy ran back to the tide pool. He remembered how seagulls swooped down to the waters after fish and carried them off in their claws. He had seen them flying off through the air with a fish many times, and he didn't want any seagull to eat his sleepy little fish, his little blue and green fish.

"Shoo, Seagull! Shoo!"

He waved his arms to show the seagull he meant what he said.

Meanwhile the tide was coming in. Icy green over the black rocks. The waves splashed louder and louder. But still the seagull wheeled screaming in the sky.

So Tommy stayed and guarded his poky fish in the tide pool. He stayed until the spray blew into his face and the sun was much nearer the edge of the ocean. Still the seagull wheeled and floated in the sky above him.

His mother came calling him, because it was time to go home. But when he showed her his fish in the pool and the hungry seagull in the sky, she sat down on the rocks beside him; and they watched the tide come in together.

It was not very long before the first wave came bursting and spilling over the edge of the rocks into the tide pool. It came farther than any of the other waves, cold over Tommy's bare foot.

But still the seagull wheeled in the sky, making hungry screaming seagull noises. Sometimes it swooped down very close to them and they had to call out, "Shoo, Seagull, shoo!"

Tommy and his mother stayed until the tide came sweeping in, wave after wave, so far that Tommy's mother had to move farther up on the rocks to keep from getting splashed. But Tommy stayed there by his tide pool until the water was around his feet. Then he, too, went up and sat down on the warm dry rocks with his mother and watched the tide come up over the tide pool and past it over the rocks.

When the tide pool was under the ocean again, they went home across the rocks. And the seagull went away in the air. And the little fish swam away through the ocean.

The Substitute

by Beverly Cleary

Something is very wrong at Ramona's kindergarten, and she's not going to put up with it. Find out what she does in this story from Ramona the Pest, *the first of many books about this rambunctious, lovable girl.*

Before long Mrs. Quimby and Mrs. Kemp decided the time had come for Ramona and Howie to walk to school by themselves. Mrs. Kemp, pushing Willa Jean in her stroller, walked Howie to the Quimbys' house, where Ramona's mother invited her in for a cup of coffee.

"You better put all your stuff away," Howie advised Ramona, as his mother lifted his little sister out of the stroller. "Willa Jean crawls around and chews things."

Grateful for this advice, Ramona closed the door of her room.

"Now, Howie, you be sure to look both ways before you cross the street," cautioned his mother.

"You, too, Ramona," said Mrs. Quimby. "And be sure you walk. And walk on the sidewalk. Don't go running out in the street."

"And cross between the white lines," said Mrs. Kemp.

"And wait for the traffic boy near the school," said Mrs. Quimby.

"And don't talk to strangers," said Mrs. Kemp.

Ramona and Howie, weighed down by the responsibility of walking themselves to school, trudged off down the street. Howie was even gloomier than usual, because he was the only boy in the morning kindergarten who wore jeans with only one hip pocket. All the other boys had two hip pockets.

"That's silly," said Ramona, still inclined to be impatient with Howie. If Howie did not like his jeans, why didn't he make a great big noisy fuss about them?

"No, it isn't," contradicted Howie. "Jeans with one hip pocket are babyish."

At the cross street Ramona and Howie stopped and looked both ways. They saw a car coming a block away so they waited. They waited and waited. When the car finally passed, they saw another car coming a block away in the opposite direction. They waited some more. At last the coast was clear, and they walked, stiff-legged in their haste, across the street. "Whew!" said Howie, relieved that they were safely across.

The next intersection was easier because Henry Huggins, in his red traffic sweater and yellow cap, was the traffic boy on duty. Ramona was not awed by Henry even though he often got to hold up cement and lumber trucks delivering material for the market that was being built across from the school. She had known Henry and his dog, Ribsy, as long as she could remember, and she admired Henry because not only was he a traffic boy, he also delivered papers.

Now Ramona looked at Henry, who was standing with his feet apart and his hands clasped behind his back. Ribsy was sitting beside him as if he were watching traffic, too. Just to see what Henry would do, Ramona stepped off the curb.

"You get back on the curb, Ramona," Henry ordered above the noise of the construction on the corner.

Ramona set one foot back on the curb.

"All the way, Ramona," said Henry.

Ramona stood with both heels on the curb, but her toes out over the gutter. Henry could not say she was not standing on the curb, so he merely glared. When several boys and girls were waiting to cross the street, Henry marched across with Ribsy prancing along beside him.

"Beat it, Ribsy," said Henry between his teeth. Ribsy paid no attention.

Directly in front of Ramona Henry executed a sharp about-face like a real soldier. Ramona marched behind Henry, stepping as close to his sneakers as she could. The other children laughed.

On the opposite curb Henry tried to execute another military about-face, but instead he tripped over Ramona. "Doggone you, Ramona," he said angrily. "If you don't cut that out I'm going to report you."

"Nobody reports kindergarteners," scoffed an older boy.

"Well, I'm going to report Ramona if she doesn't cut it out," said Henry. Obviously Henry felt it was his bad luck that he had to guard an intersection where Ramona crossed the street.

Between crossing the street without a grown-up and getting so much attention from Henry, Ramona felt that her day was off to a good start. However, as she and Howie approached the kindergarten building, she saw at once that something was wrong. The door to the kindergarten was already open. No one was playing on the jungle gym. No one was running around the playground. No one was even waiting in line by the door. Instead the boys and girls were huddled in groups like frightened mice. They all looked worried and once in a while someone who appeared to be acting brave would run to the open door, peer inside, and come running back to one of the groups to report something.

"What's the matter?" asked Ramona.

"Miss Binney isn't there," whispered Susan. "It's a different lady."

"A substitute," said Eric R.

Miss Binney not there! Susan must be wrong. Miss Binney had to be there. Kindergarten would not be kindergarten without Miss Binney. Ramona ran to the door to see for herself. Susan was right. Miss Binney was not there. The woman who was busy at Miss Binney's desk was taller and older. She was as old as a mother. Her dress was brown and her shoes were sensible.

Ramona did not like what she saw at all, so she ran back to a cluster of boys and girls. "What are we going to do?" she asked, feeling as if she had been deserted by Miss Binney. For her teacher to go home and not come back was not right.

"I think I'll go home," said Susan.

Ramona thought this idea was babyish of Susan. She had seen what happened to boys and girls who ran home from kindergarten. Their mothers marched them right straight back again, that's what happened. No, going home would not do.

"I bet the substitute won't even know the rules of our kindergarten," said Howie.

The children agreed. Miss Binney said following the rules of their kindergarten was important. How could this stranger know what the rules were? A stranger would not even know the names of the boys and girls. She might get them mixed up.

Still feeling that Miss Binney was disloyal to stay away from school, Ramona made up her mind she was not going into that kindergarten room with that strange teacher. Nobody could make her go in there. But where could she go? She could not go home, because her mother would march her back. She could not go into the main building of Glenwood School, because everyone would know a girl her size belonged out in the kindergarten. She had to hide, but where?

When the first bell rang, Ramona knew she did not have much time. There was no place to hide on the kindergarten playground, so she slipped around behind the little building and joined the boys and girls who were streaming into the red-brick building.

"Kindergarten baby!" a first grader shouted at Ramona.

"Pieface!" answered Ramona with spirit. She could see only two places to hide — behind the bicycle racks or behind a row of trash cans. Ramona chose the trash cans. As the last children entered the building she got down on her hands and knees and crawled into the space between the cans and the red-brick wall.

The second bell rang. "Hup, two, three, four! Hup, two, three, four!" The traffic boys were marching back from their posts at the intersections near the school. Ramona crouched motionless on the asphalt. "Hup, two, three, four!" The traffic boys, heads up, eyes front, marched past the trash cans and into the building. The playground was quiet, and Ramona was alone.

Henry's dog, Ribsy, who had followed the traffic boys as far as the door of the school, came trotting over to check the odors of the trash cans. He put his nose down to the ground and whiffled around the cans while Ramona crouched motionless with the rough asphalt digging into her knees. Ribsy's busy nose led him around the can face to face with Ramona.

"Wuf!" said Ribsy.

"Ribsy, go away!" ordered Ramona in a whisper.

"R–r–r–wuf!" Ribsy knew Ramona was not supposed to be behind the trash cans.

"You be quiet!" Ramona's whisper was as ferocious as she could make it. Over in the kindergarten the class began to sing the song about the dawnzer. At least the strange woman knew that much about kindergarten. After the dawnzer song the kindergarten was quiet. Ramona wondered if the teacher knew that Show-and-Tell was supposed to come next. She strained her ears, but she could not hear any activity in the little building.

The space between the brick wall and the trash cans began to feel as cold as a refrigerator to Ramona in her thin sweater. The asphalt dug into her knees, so she sat down with her feet straight out toward Ribsy's nose. The minutes dragged by.

Except for Ribsy, Ramona was lonely. She leaned against the chill red bricks and felt sorry for herself. Poor little Ramona, all alone except for Ribsy, behind the trash cans. Miss Binney would be sorry if she knew what she had made Ramona do. She would be sorry if she knew how cold and lonesome Ramona was. Ramona felt so sorry for the poor shivering little child behind the trash cans that one tear and then another slid down her cheeks. She sniffed pitifully. Ribsy opened one eye and looked at her before he closed it again. Not even Henry's dog cared what happened to her.

After a while Ramona heard the kindergarten running and laughing outside. How disloyal everyone was to have so much fun when Miss Binney had deserted her class. Ramona wondered if the kindergarten missed her and if anyone else would chase Davy and try to kiss him. Then Ramona must have dozed off, because the next thing she knew recess time had come and the playground was swarming with shouting, yelling, ball-throwing older boys and girls. Ribsy was gone. Stiff with cold, Ramona hunched down as low as she could. A ball bounced with a bang against a trash can. Ramona shut her eyes and hoped that if she could not see anyone, no one could see her.

Footsteps came running toward the ball. "Hey!" exclaimed a boy's voice. "There's a little kid hiding back here!"

Ramona's eyes flew open. "Go away!" she said fiercely to the strange boy, who was peering over the cans at her.

"What are you hiding back there for?" asked the boy.

"*Go away!*" ordered Ramona.

"Hey, Huggins!" yelled the boy. "There's a little kid back here who lives over near you!"

In a moment Henry was peering over the trash cans at Ramona. "What are you doing there?" he demanded. "You're supposed to be in kindergarten."

"You mind your own business," said Ramona.

Naturally when two boys peered behind the trash cans, practically the whole school had to join them to see what was so interesting. "What's she doing?" people asked. "How come she's hiding?" "Does her teacher know she's here?"

In the midst of all the excitement, Ramona felt a new discomfort.

"Find her sister," someone said. "Get Beatrice. She'll know what to do."

No one had to find Beezus. She was already there. "Ramona Geraldine Quimby!" she said. "You come out of there this minute!"

"I won't," said Ramona, even though she knew she could not stay there much longer.

"Ramona, you just wait until Mother hears about this!" stormed Beezus. "You're really going to catch it!"

133

Ramona knew that Beezus was right, but catching it from her mother was not what was worrying her at the moment.

"Here comes the yard teacher," someone said.

Ramona had to admit defeat. She got to her hands and knees and then to her feet and faced the crowd across the trash-can lids as the yard teacher came to investigate the commotion.

"Don't you belong in kindergarten?" the yard teacher asked.

"I'm not going to go to kindergarten," said Ramona stubbornly, and cast an anguished glance at Beezus.

"She's supposed to be in kindergarten," said Beezus, "but she needs to go to the bathroom." The older boys and girls thought this remark was funny, which made Ramona so angry she wanted to cry. There was nothing funny about it at all, and if she didn't hurry —

The yard teacher turned to Beezus. "Take her to the bathroom and then to the principal's office. She'll find out what the trouble is."

The first words were a relief to Ramona, but the second a shock. No one in the morning kindergarten had ever been sent to Miss Mullen's office in the big building, except to deliver a note from Miss Binney, and then the children went in pairs, because the errand was such a scary one. "What will the principal do to me?" Ramona asked, as Beezus led her away to the girl's bathroom in the big building.

"I don't know," said Beezus. "Talk to you, I guess, or call Mother. Ramona, why did you have to go and do a dumb thing like hiding behind the trash cans?"

"Because." Ramona was cross since Beezus was so cross. When the girls came out of the bathroom, Ramona reluctantly allowed herself to be led into the principal's office, where she felt small and frightened even though she tried not to show it.

"This is my little sister, Ramona," Beezus explained to Miss Mullen's secretary in the outer office. "She belongs in kindergarten, but she's been hiding behind the trash cans."

Miss Mullen must have overheard, because she came out of her office. Frightened though she was, Ramona braced herself to say, I won't go back to kindergarten!

"Why, hello, Ramona," said Miss Mullen. "That's all right, Beatrice. You may go back to your class. I'll take over."

Ramona wanted to stay close to her sister, but Beezus walked out of the office, leaving her alone with the principal, the most important person in the whole school. Ramona felt small and pitiful with her knees still marked where the asphalt had gouged her. Miss Mullen smiled, as if Ramona's behavior was of no particular importance, and said, "Isn't it too bad Miss Binney had to stay home with a sore throat? I know what a surprise it was for you to find a strange teacher in your kindergarten room."

Ramona wondered how Miss Mullen knew so much. The principal did not even bother to ask what Ramona was doing behind the trash cans. She did not feel the least bit sorry for the poor little girl with the gouged knees. She simply took Ramona by the hand, and said, "I'm going to introduce you to Mrs. Wilcox. I know you're going to like her," and started out the door.

Ramona felt a little indignant, because Miss Mullen did not demand to know why she had been hiding all that time. Miss Mullen did not even notice how forlorn and tearstained Ramona looked. Ramona had been so cold and lonely and miserable that she thought Miss Mullen should show some interest. She had half expected the principal to say, Why, you poor little thing! Why were you hiding behind the trash cans?

The looks on the faces of the morning kindergarten, when

Ramona walked into the room with the principal, made up for Miss Mullen's lack of concern. Round eyes, open mouths, faces blank with surprise — Ramona was delighted to see the whole class staring at her from their seats. *They* were worried about her. *They* cared what had happened to her.

"Ramona, this is Miss Binney's substitute, Mrs. Wilcox," said Miss Mullen. To the substitute she said, "Ramona is a little late this morning." That was all. Not a word about how cold and miserable Ramona had been. Not a word about how brave she had been to hide until recess.

"I'm glad you're here, Ramona," said Mrs. Wilcox, as the principal left. "The class is drawing with crayons. What would you like to draw?"

Here it was seat-work time, and Mrs. Wilcox was not even having the class do real seat work, but was letting them draw pictures as if this day were the first day of kindergarten. Ramona was most disapproving. Things were not supposed to be this way. She looked at Howie scrubbing away with a blue crayon to make a sky across the top of his paper and at Davy, who was drawing a man whose arms seemed to come out of his ears. They were busy and happy drawing whatever they pleased.

"I would like to make Q's," said Ramona on sudden inspiration.

"Make use of what?" asked Mrs. Wilcox, holding out a sheet of drawing paper.

Ramona had been sure all along that the substitute could not be as smart as Miss Binney, but at least she expected her to know what the letter Q was. All grown-ups were supposed to know Q. "Nothing," Ramona said, as she accepted the paper and, pleasantly self-conscious under the awed stares of the kindergarten, went to her seat.

At last Ramona was free to draw her Q her own way. Forget-ting the loneliness and discomfort of the morning, she drew a most satisfying row of Q's, Ramona-style, and decided that hav-ing a substitute teacher was not so bad after all.

ϙ ϙ ϙ ϙ ϙ ϙ ϙ

Mrs. Wilcox wandered up and down the aisle looking at pic-tures. "Why, Ramona," she said, pausing by Ramona's desk, "what charming little cats you've drawn! Do you have kittens at home?"

Ramona felt sorry for poor Mrs. Wilcox, a grown-up lady teacher who did not know Q. "No," she answered. "Our cat is a boy cat."

Dumpling Soup

by Jama Kim Rattigan

Join in the fun as Marisa and her extended family celebrate the New Year in Hawaii.

Every year on New Year's Eve, my whole family goes to Grandma's house for dumpling soup. My aunties and uncles and cousins come from all around Oahu. Most of them are Korean, but some are Japanese, Chinese, Hawaiian, or *haole* (Hawaiian for white people). Grandma calls our family "chop suey," which means "all mixed up" in pidgin. I like it that way. So does Grandma. "More spice," she says.

This year, since I am seven, Grandma says I can help make dumplings, too. Everybody in my family *loves* to eat, so we have to make lots *and lots* of dumplings.

The night before New Year's Eve, Grandma, Auntie Elsie, Auntie Ruth, and Auntie Grace come to our house to work on the filling. My mother has bought great big piles of beef, pork, and vegetables to fill the dumplings and special dumpling wrappers from the Gum Chew Lau Noodle Factory in Honolulu. Everyone brings her own cleaver and cutting board and sits at the kitchen table, chopping and talking, chopping and talking, late into the night.

"Too much gossip!" says Grandma in Korean. "Mince that cabbage! More bean sprouts!" It is her recipe, so she is very picky.

"What about me?" I want to help.

"Tomorrow, Marisa," answers Grandma. "You can help us wrap."

So tonight I watch Grandma mix everything in a big metal pan — more tofu, more onion, more salt, more soy sauce. My aunties keep working, and I fall asleep listening to the *chop-chop* pounding, *chop-scrape-scrape*. Later, when my mother wakes me up to go to bed, her hands smell like garlic.

The next morning, I am the first one up. I wake up my brother, Hiram. Then together we tiptoe to my mother and father's room.

"Get up, get up! It's New Year's Eve! We have to go to Grandma's to wrap the *mandoo*."

"Not yet," my mother says with her eyes still closed.

"Please wait till the sun comes up," says my father.

But we are too excited to sleep. Today, everyone will be at Grandma's. We will see cousins we haven't seen all year, and we will stay up all night. Hiram will help my uncles with the fireworks. But best of all, I will learn to wrap dumplings for dumpling soup.

When we finally get to Grandma's, other aunts who live near Wahiawa have already started wrapping. All of Auntie Faye's dumplings are rectangles, and she lines them up like soldiers. Auntie Ruth pinches her dumplings along the edges to make them look fancy. Auntie Grace puts more filling in the middle than anyone else. "I like fat ones," she says.

"Okay, Marisa, these are for you." Grandma places a small stack of wrappers in front of me. My mother pushes her bowl of finger-dipping water closer.

I want to make good dumplings. I want to show my aunties. I try to copy them, but sometimes I put too much filling in the middle. Sometimes I don't put enough water along the edges. My dumplings look a little funny, not perfect like the ones my aunts have made. What if no one wants to eat them? I feel Grandma's hand on my shoulder and look up.

"*Cha-koo hae bo-ra,* Marisa." I don't understand all of Grandma's Korean, but I can tell by her face what she's saying: "Don't worry — keep trying."

Soon there are trays and trays of beautifully wrapped dumplings all over the kitchen. They look like hundreds of baby bottoms wrapped in diapers, powdered on the outside. Mine look a little sad, all different lumpy shapes. One by one, my mother tosses all of them into Grandma's biggest pot full of boiling water.

When the dumplings are cooked, they float up, wrinkled and shiny. Grandma calls my father for the official taste test. No one knows spices like he does. He bites into one of the cooled dumplings, chews slowly, and wrinkles his forehead.

"What, too *mae wo?*" ("Too spicy hot?") My mother is anxious. "*Seen gu wa?*" ("Not enough salt?") "Or *jaah?*" ("Too salty?")

He gobbles up the rest of the dumpling, smiling and nodding. "Mmmm! *Ono!!* One more to make sure."

I watch the pot carefully for my dumplings. There they are! But some float up without their wrappers. And others look like they lost their filling. Grandma scoops all of them into a colander to cool.

"We'll eat your *mandoo* later," she tells me.

But I worry that they are bad *mandoo* and that no one will want to eat them. Is Grandma putting them away so they won't spoil the soup? Maybe it's bad luck to eat ugly dumplings on New Year's.

Before I can ask her, more relatives knock on the door. They come from far away, from Kaneohe, Kahala, and Waialae. Now Wahiawa, which means "place of noise" in Hawaiian, becomes a place of *big* noise.

I hold the screen door open for all the aunties carrying heaping plates of food. "Watch out! Coming through!" They bring homemade *sushi, jhun,* and *sashimi.*

Auntie Mori arrives last with a special treat: Japanese *mochi*. She says *mochi-ii* means "to stay in your stomach for a long time." *Mochi-zuki* means "full moon." The little cakes do look like white moons, and the sweet, chewy bites feel so good in our stomachs.

"*Mochi* help keep the family stuck together!" Uncle Myung Ho says after swallowing seven in a row.

More cars drive up. Now they line the whole street. By six o'clock, Grandma's front steps are covered with big, medium, and little slippers, sandals, and shoes. So many Yangs!

New Year's Eve is the only night in the whole year we are allowed to stay up all night. Grandma told us that in Korea, if you fell asleep before midnight, your eyebrows would turn snowy white. But staying awake is easy for us. We never run out of games.

"Let's hug Grandma!" shouts my *haole* cousin, Maxie. This is our favorite game. We line up in front of Grandma. When it is my turn, I stretch my arms to reach around her bouncy, soft tummy and then rest my head against it. She laughs, and my head bobs up and down. My grandma is like a warm pillow.

Inside and out, everyone finds something fun to do. We play a game we can play only on New Year's: shoe store. We go to the front steps. "I'll be the shoe store lady!" shouts Carrie. The rest of us take turns trying on all our favorite styles.

"Do you have these gold slippers in size fifty and a half?" asks Maxie.

"Aren't these red high heels just *perfect* with my muumuu?" Alicia shows off.

After a while, all the slippers and shoes get mixed up and seem to be walking all over Grandma's yard. Since it has gotten so late, we really should pick them up. But we're too tired.

❖   ❖   ❖

When it is almost midnight, we hear Hiram and the older cousins running to poke big sparklers into the grass.

"Somebody check the clock!" orders Hiram. Alicia presses her face against the screen door.

"Twelve minutes to twelve!" she yells. All of a sudden it is almost time, and everybody moves quickly.

From every corner of the house the Yangs come. Everyone finds a place to stand on the cool grass. All the cousins gather under the litchi tree. The babies rub their eyes and whine. My Chinese cousin, Helen, says fireworks scare away the evil spirits. We want good luck in the coming year. Grandma takes one last look around to make sure everyone is there.

For a moment, the only sound is the shush of the *hapuu* plants. "Good-bye, Old Year," I whisper.

Finally we count down the seconds till midnight: Five, four, three, two, one . . .

"Happy New Year!"

Thousands of firecrackers explode, filling the sky with smoke. All up and down Grandma's street, there is popping and snapping. Our eyes water and our ears ring. Hiram and I run to light all the sparklers, then write our names in the night sky. Cousins, aunts, uncles, brothers, sisters, and friends hug and shake hands.

Finally, Grandma calls, *"Ppalli! Mo-gup-sida!"* Time for *dumpling soup!*

"If we eat first thing on New Year's Day, we won't go hungry for the rest of the year," my father reminds us. The table is set with deep bowls and big spoons.

"Eh!" says Uncle Myung Ho. "What kind *mandoo* this?" I quickly look in some of the bowls. Oh, no! Grandma has put one of my funny-looking dumplings in each!

"Must be the ones Risa made," says Hiram. "They look like little elephant ears."

Everybody laughs. My face feels hot.

Uncle Myung Ho blows on his spoon and takes a bite. *"Ono, Marisa!* Delicious!"

145

Grandma walks over. Her bowl is full of my *mandoo!*

"I've been waiting all night to taste these," she says. "Here, have one." She puts another funny-looking triangle in my bowl.

We bite into our dumplings at the same time.

"*Ai-go chŭm!*" she says. "This is the best *mandoo* I have ever tasted!"

I finish my funny-looking dumpling. Mmmm! Grandma's right! It is good! The spices tickle my tongue.

"Who wants more of Marisa's *mandoo?*" Grandma asks. Everybody holds out his bowl. I hold out my bowl, too. More dumplings! More lip-smacking chicken broth! Warm, steamy, and delicious!

With our dumplings, we eat roast pork, three kinds of *kimchi,* spinach and bean sprout *namul,* spicy seaweed, *taegu,* boiled tripe,

and octopus. Hiram and I love the Korean dessert we get only on New Year's: *yak pap*. He pulls off a chunk of the brown sticky rice mixed with honey, dates, and pine nuts and hands it to me. I lick every bit off my fingers.

"Your elephant ears sure tasted better than they looked!" he says to me.

I think about how much everyone liked the dumpling soup. Even my funny dumplings. Maybe it was because we ate them at Grandma's, all of us together.

"Next year," I tell everyone, "I will make even *better* dumplings."

I can hardly wait.

Hello, brand-new year!

ACKNOWLEDGMENTS

*Grateful acknowledgment is made to the following authors, agents,
and publishers for permission to reprint the stories listed below.*

Margaret Wise Brown:
"The Fish That Got Left in the Tide Pool," by Margaret Wise Brown, from *Another Here and Now Story Book,* by Lucy Sprague Mitchell. Copyright 1937 by E. P. Dutton, renewed © 1965 by Lucy Sprague Mitchell. Reprinted by permission of Dutton Children's Books, a division of Penguin Books USA Inc.

Ann Cameron:
"A Curve in the River," from *More Stories Julian Tells,* by Ann Cameron. Copyright © 1986 by Ann Cameron. Reprinted by permission of Random House, Inc.

Beverly Cleary:
"The Substitute," from *Ramona the Pest,* by Beverly Cleary. Copyright © 1968 by Beverly Cleary. Reprinted by permission of Morrow Junior Books, a division of William Morrow & Company, Inc.

Kristine L. Franklin:
"Abuelo's House," by Kristine L. Franklin. Copyright © 1992 by Kristine L. Franklin.

Wanda Gág:
"Clever Elsie," from *Tales from Grimm,* retold by Wanda Gág, copyright 1936 by Wanda Gág, © renewed 1964 by Robert Janssen. Reprinted by permission of Coward-McCann, Inc., a division of The Putnam Publishing Group.

Barbara Giles:
"Maria's Invisible Cat," by Barbara Giles, from *The Viking Bedtime Treasury,* compiled and edited by Rosalind Price & Walter McVitty. Copyright © 1987 by The Macquarie Library Pty Ltd. Reprinted by permission of Penguin Books Australia Ltd.

Virginia Haviland:
"Rumpelstiltskin," from *Favorite Fairy Tales from Around the World,* retold by Virginia Haviland. Copyright © 1959 by Virginia Haviland. By permission of Little, Brown and Company.

Barbara Shook Hazen:
"The Sorcerer's Apprentice," adapted by Barbara Shook Hazen. Copyright © 1969 by Barbara Shook Hazen. Reprinted by permission of Gotham Art & Literary Agency, Inc.

Johanna Hurwitz:
"Nora the Baby-Sitter," from *Busybody Nora,* by Johanna Hurwitz. Copyright © 1976 by Johanna Hurwitz. Reprinted by permission of Morrow Junior Books, a division of William Morrow & Company, Inc.

Jean Van Leeuwen:
"The Monster," from *Tales of Amanda Pig,* by Jean Van Leeuwen. Copyright © 1983 by Jean Van Leeuwen. Reprinted by permission of Dial Books for Young Readers, a division of Penguin Books USA Inc.

Alice Low:
"The Quilted Elephant and the Green Plush Dragon," by Alice Low. Copyright © 1991, 1996 by Alice Low. Reprinted by permission of the author.

Betty MacDonald:
"The Radish Cure," from *Mrs. Piggle-Wiggle,* by Betty MacDonald. Copyright © 1957 by Betty MacDonald. Reprinted by permission of HarperCollins Publishers.

Jama Kim Rattigan:
Dumpling Soup, by Jama Kim Rattigan. Text copyright © 1993 by Jama Kim Rattigan. By permission of Little, Brown and Company.

James Riordan:
"The Squire's Bride," by James Riordan, from *The Woman in the Moon,* by James Riordan, illustrated by Angela Barrett. Copyright © 1984 by James Riordan. Reprinted by permission of Dial Books for Young Readers, a division of Penguin Books USA Inc., and by Hutchinson Children's Books.

Louis Sachar:
"Paul," from *Sideways Stories from Wayside School,* by Louis Sachar. Copyright © 1978 by Louis Sachar. Reprinted by permission of Avon Books.

Howard Schwartz and Barbara Rush:
"The Prince Who Thought He Was a Rooster," from *The Diamond Tree,* by Howard Schwartz and Barbara Rush. Copyright © 1991 by Howard Schwartz and Barbara Rush. Reprinted by permission of HarperCollins Publishers.

P. L. Travers:
"The Day Out," from *Mary Poppins,* by P. L. Travers. Copyright 1934 and © renewed 1962 by P. L. Travers. Reprinted by permission of Harcourt Brace & Company.

The following stories have been retold and first published in this volume: *Molly Whuppie,* retold from Joseph Jacobs, copyright © 1996 by Alice Low; and *Lazy Jack,* retold from Joseph Jacobs, copyright © 1996 by Little, Brown and Company.